M

Miracles

A job exchange b... ...the most innovative neonatal clinics in the world throws brother-and-sister dream team Dr. Kirri and Dr. Lucas West completely out of their comfort zones.

As Kirri heads to Atlanta and Lucas welcomes a new colleague in Sydney, they're going to be miles apart but helping to bring joy and longed-for families to so many more with their new working partnerships.

Only, while they are used to making baby miracles with the help of cutting-edge science, the miracles *they're* about to receive have little to do with science…and everything to do with love!

Discover Kirri's story in
Risking Her Heart on the Single Dad

And find Lucas's story in
The Neonatal Doc's Baby Surprise

Both available now!

Dear Reader,

When I was asked to write this duet with the fabulous Annie O'Neil, I jumped at the chance. When we picked Atlanta and Sydney as the settings, I snatched up Sydney. I love the city. I had a chance to pretend I was Amanda visiting the sites and living at Lucius's glorious home. I have to admit that I became caught up in the story. I hope you do, too.

I want to thank the Atlanta Center for Reproductive Medicine for being kind enough to answer over the phone a crazy stranger's odd question. I'm also grateful to Rachel Jones, a fellow Georgia romance writer and retired labor and delivery nurse, for making suggestions for major issues during delivery.

As always, I love to hear from you. Contact me at susancarlisle.com.

Susan

THE NEONATAL DOC'S
BABY SURPRISE

SUSAN CARLISLE

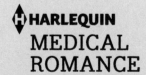

HARLEQUIN
MEDICAL
ROMANCE

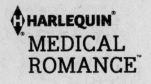

HARLEQUIN®
MEDICAL ROMANCE™

Recycling programs
for this product may
not exist in your area.

ISBN-13: 978-1-335-14936-7

The Neonatal Doc's Baby Surprise

Harlequin Enterprises ULC
22 Adelaide St. West, 40th Floor
Toronto, Ontario M5H 4E3, Canada
www.Harlequin.com

Printed in U.S.A.

Susan Carlisle's love affair with books began in the sixth grade, when she made a bad grade in mathematics. Not allowed to watch TV until she'd brought the grade up, Susan filled her time with books. She turned her love of reading into a passion for writing, and now has over ten Harlequin Medical Romance novels published. She writes about hot, sexy docs and the strong women who captivate them. Visit susancarlisle.com.

Books by Susan Carlisle

Harlequin Medical Romance

First Response
Firefighter's Unexpected Fling

Pups that Make Miracles
Highland Doc's Christmas Rescue

Christmas in Manhattan
Christmas with the Best Man

Stolen Kisses with Her Boss
Redeeming the Rebel Doc
The Brooding Surgeon's Baby Bombshell
A Daddy Sent by Santa
Nurse to Forever Mom
The Sheikh Doc's Marriage Bargain

Visit the Author Profile page
at Harlequin.com for more titles.

Thanks for our years of friendship. Love you.
War Eagle!

**Praise for
Susan Carlisle**

CHAPTER ONE

AMANDA LONGSTREET PULLED her large suitcase behind her as she exited the Kingsford Smith Airport in Sydney, Australia. The heated air touching her skin put the winter weather of Atlanta, Georgia, well behind her. She enjoyed traveling but she had never gone this far. Twenty-two hours in a small seat flanked by two strangers hadn't been as much fun as she'd envisioned, but still the excitement of coming to Sydney grew within her.

She was counting on the destination making up for the discomforts of the flight. The Piedmont Women and Baby Pavilion, where she worked back in Atlanta, would have probably paid for a first-class ticket for her, but she was too practical to ask. She'd much rather see the money spent on helping a couple wanting a baby.

Making her way across the street to the pickup area, she remained mindful that in this country they drove on the opposite side of the road. Some people called it the wrong side, but it really wasn't—it was just different. She located the sign for airport pickup and stood beneath it, waiting for her car to arrive.

She scanned the area and harrumphed. Dr. Kirri West had told her Sydney was an amazing city. So far it looked like any other big airport.

Jet lag was no doubt affecting Amanda's attitude. Given a few days, and a chance to explore, she'd surely agree with Kirri's opinion. Right now, all she wanted was to get to her apartment—home for the next six weeks—and crawl into bed.

Still, excitement sizzled in her. She anticipated checking out the city, but only after she'd had some rest and started her job at the clinic. After all, the experience of working at the Harborside Fertility and Neonatal Centre had been the reason she'd come here.

Sighing, she looked up and then down the paved area. *Where was the car?* Her contact at the clinic had said there would be one coming for her. She was past ready for it to arrive.

Patience wasn't her virtue. More than once her mother and friends had told her that her life plan wasn't the be all and end all of existence. That she should lighten up a little.

Even with that advice in mind she'd tucked into her purse a list of things she wanted to do and see in Sydney. As a child, she'd been just as focused on her goals. She had a plan for her life. So far she'd remained on track. In every aspect but one.

Amanda pushed her hair out of her face. Having the chance to work with Kirri had been a real pleasure, but to be under the tutelage of Kirri's brother would only help Amanda rise in her profession. She'd heard enough about Dr. Lucius West from Kirri to know he was a focused and exacting doctor, who had little time for anything but his work. He sounded like a doctor who liked things done by the book. They should get along well.

Where was this car? Was she waiting in the wrong place?

Amanda checked the sign once more. She paced down the sidewalk and then back again, squinting into the sunshine. Had she misunderstood the instructions?

A few minutes later, to her great relief, a black car with the clinic's logo on the door pulled to a stop beside her.

She smiled as the driver climbed out.

"Ms. Longstreet?" A ruddy-faced, heavy-set man came around the back of the car.

"Yes."

"I'm here to pick you up." He pushed a button and popped the trunk lid, taking her luggage.

"I'm glad to see you."

He gave her a brief smile, stowed her suitcase in the trunk, and then opened the passenger door. While she settled in he quickly returned to the driver's seat, and they were soon moving.

She shivered. The air-conditioning blasted cold air. At least it would help keep her awake long enough to get to the apartment.

A swift movement outside the car caught her attention. A blond-haired man with long determined strides was hurrying toward the car. He carried a satchel over one shoulder and pulled along a small overnight bag. His suit jacket was slung over one arm and his tie had been pulled away from his neck. It lay twisted and askew, as if he had done it in frustration.

Her heart jumped.

Dr. Lucius West. She recognized him from her internet research on the Sydney clinic.

He raised his hand and the driver pulled to the curb. After a rapid tap on the front passenger window the driver lowered it. Dr. West glanced at her with tight-lipped agitation. He said to the driver, "I'm Dr. West. I expected you thirty minutes ago. Why are you late?"

Amanda sighed. She was too tired for this drama. Maybe Kirri hadn't been exaggerating about her brother.

"Yes, sir. I was on my way to you." The driver nodded his head toward Amanda. "I had another pickup to make first."

Dr. West didn't wait for the driver to get out and open the door for him. Instead he deposited his bag in the front seat and joined her in the back. Amanda quickly moved across the seat, fearing that if she didn't he would sit in her lap. The space shrank with him inside. She hadn't expected he'd be such a *large* man.

In addition to that unsettling fact, his pictures hadn't done him justice. He was far better-looking in person. A sliver of silver at his temples in his wavy blond hair shimmered in the sunlight, giving him a distinguished look. One that meshed with his reputation and position. On one of the websites she'd seen he had made the shortlist of most eligible bachelors in Australia. Amanda wasn't surprised. She couldn't help but be awestruck and stare.

"You are...?" he demanded as he settled in, holding his satchel in his lap.

"Amanda Longstreet."

Dr. West studied her for a moment. His eyes were a deep blue, like the ocean, instead of bright blue like his sister's. There were creases at the corners and telltale dark smudges below. Had he been on a flight as long as hers?

"You're American." His words were flat, as if he were determining a diagnosis.

"I am."

Why didn't he recognize her name? Hadn't he been told she was coming?

He continued to study her, as if trying to pull up something that was filed away in his mind.

He nodded slowly. "Ah, yes, I remember now. You're the clinical nurse specialist in the exchange program. Kirri mentioned you."

He *should* remember, since he had been one of the doctors to start it. His clinic and the clinic where she worked were two of the most prestigious and innovative in their care for mother and baby, with a special emphasis on infertility issues. Dr. Lucius West, along with Dr. Sawyer, the head of her clinic, had decided during a conference that a staff exchange to share information would be productive for both clinics. Kirri had come to Atlanta for six weeks and now, it was Amanda's turn.

She gave him her sunniest smile. "Yes, that's me."

He continued to watch her. "I'm Lucius West."

"Yes, I know. You resemble your sister." And she had ogled his picture on the computer screen more than once. "It's nice to meet you."

The opportunity to work with the world-renowned Dr. Lucius West would be the honor of a lifetime. Although Kirri had warned Amanda that her brother could be difficult. She had already started to see signs of that!

"Mmm." His attention remained on the electronic tablet he'd pulled from his satchel. "I'm sorry, I have work to attend to."

"I understand."

She did. He was the head of the clinic and she knew he must have many demands on his time.

A short while later Lucius glanced at the pretty woman huddled in the seat corner with her arms across her chest and her eyes closed. Was she asleep?

He'd forgotten all about the person coming from Atlanta for the staff exchange. It had been mentioned during one of the recent staff meetings, but he'd been checking his emails, only half listening. He'd paid no mind to the date and time of her arrival.

Not that it really mattered, but he had expected a man. Although the gender of the person was of no consequence, since he had little to do with the staff in Labor and Delivery. If he remembered correctly, that was where she would be assigned.

Giving her a closer look, he found her attractive enough, with short brown hair, clear skin and a faint tan. Her figure of full curves instead of bony angles enhanced her appeal. She wore little make-up—but that might be because she'd been on a plane for hours.

Further testimony to how drained she must be feeling was in the dark smudges that shadowed her eyes. Those green eyes which had brightened when she'd realized who he was. All in all she made for an interesting package—if he had been looking for one.

Despite her clear anticipation of working with him, he doubted he'd have much contact with her during her visit. He spent most of his time on the in vitro side of the clinic—not where she would be working. He did follow a few cases from start to finish, but there were many others on the staff who handled ninety-nine percent of the deliveries.

It would be awkward when she woke. He couldn't remember her name...

Amanda. That was it.

He mentally rolled the name around for a second. Had he ever known an Amanda? Not that he could remember.

He looked at her again. Her hair curtained her face. In her sleep she slumped further into the corner, with her chin falling to her chest. She appeared uncomfortable.

Leaning toward her, he eased his arm around her back, pulling her upright with gentleness until her head rested on his shoulder. She released a small sigh and settled against him.

He returned to his electric pad to review his emails.

A stack of work always awaited him. He liked it that way. His work was his life. He had a major part to play in making great medical advances in infertility. Once he'd tried to have a life outside the clinic. But what had that gotten him? A shattered marriage and a disillusioned heart.

Amanda snored softly. Lucius smiled.

He was tired as well. The trip home from Melbourne after a three-day conference and a return flight delay had been topped off when his ride hadn't been waiting for him. It hadn't left him in the best of humors. Disruption of his timetable was a constant irritation. That must have shown in his manner. He undoubtedly hadn't made a good impression on his visitor.

The driver was making excellent time through

the city's afternoon traffic. It wasn't long until he pulled up in front of a small apartment complex in a neighborhood Lucius didn't know well.

"Why are we stopping here?"

"This is where your young lady gets out." The driver looked at him in the rearview mirror.

She wasn't Lucius's young lady. He hadn't had one of those since his ex-wife had walked out on him.

Lucius cupped Amanda's shoulder and shook her. "Amanda, wake up. You're here."

"Uh...?" Long dark lashes fluttered upward.

The action mesmerized him. He hadn't reacted to a woman like this in years. Not since the early years of his relationship with his ex-wife. Amanda's eyes were the green of tree leaves in early spring. And there was a sparkle in them even though she'd just awakened.

"What's wrong?"

Sleep had made her voice a little coarse. Sort of sexy.

He swallowed. That wasn't a thought he should be having about a woman he'd just met.

"Nothing. We're at your place."

Her unfocused gaze met his and he watched as reality dawned on her.

Her cheeks turned pink as she pushed at her silky hair and quickly straightened. "I'm sorry. I didn't mean to fall asleep on you."

"Hey, I've made that flight to America. I know what it takes out of you."

He gave her a sympathetic smile. Now that his sister had moved there permanently he would be going a lot more often.

Amanda returned a weak one. "That doesn't ease my embarrassment."

"No reason to be embarrassed. We're at your apartment."

Lucius opened his door to climb out. Grudgingly, he conceded that her appeal grew with her confusion. Most of the women he met never appeared ruffled, or would never admit they were. He found Amanda's obvious mortification utterly charming.

Not to mention her lovely accent…

Amanda scrambled from the car behind Lucius. The driver had placed her large suitcase on the sidewalk.

Lucius said to him, "I'll be right back. Wait for me." Then he pulled out the handle of her bulky bag and started toward the apartment building.

Stunned that this busy, world-renowned doctor planned to escort her, Amanda just stood there.

He stopped after a couple of steps and looked at her. "Well…?"

"It's not necessary for you to see me to my apartment."

"I was taught that a gentleman doesn't leave

a woman stranded on the side of the road." He grinned. "Especially one who has come so far."

Amanda blinked twice. Her first impression of him had been that he was a self-absorbed person, too busy for casual conversation. Yet he'd allowed her to sleep on his shoulder and now he was insisting on carrying her luggage like a bell hop.

Who was the real Dr. Lucius West?

"Surely the driver can help me with that?" She indicated her oversized suitcase.

"I'm sorry," the driver said as he moved back around the car. "I'm not allowed to do more than load and unload the trunk and drive. It's a liability issue."

Amanda looked at Lucius for confirmation.

He nodded.

"Oh, okay…thanks."

She followed Lucius to the apartment building entrance, conscious of the thump-thump of the tiny wheels of her heavy case on the sidewalk.

"Do you have a key, or do you have to call someone?" he asked.

"I have a key. I was sent all the information. I'm in Apartment 203."

She held the glass door open for him to enter. She looked for an elevator, and finding none led the way up the stairs. "Well, at least I'll be getting some exercise," she said.

"Yeah, and you're going to get plenty more of that at the clinic," Lucius drawled behind her.

He must have switched to the carrying handle, because she didn't hear the expected bumping of the luggage as they climbed.

"How far is the clinic from here?"

He placed the bag on the floor in front of the door with the gold numbers 203 tacked to it. "Maybe half a mile?"

"Great. That'll be a nice walk every day."

"I don't know this neighborhood well, but you'll need to be careful about being out at night by yourself. Get a ride with someone or take a taxi on late nights."

Amanda stopped searching through her purse for the door key and met his look. "I'll keep that in mind, but I'm very capable of taking care of myself."

He studied her from head to toe, then brought his gaze back to hers. "If you say so."

She wasn't sure she liked his tone. Thankfully she found the koala bear key chain and pulled it out.

"I see you've already gone native." He nodded toward her hand.

"I couldn't resist. Bought it off the Internet. I was so excited about coming to Australia."

"Is this your first time here?"

"Yes."

Amanda slid the key into the lock, turned the knob and opened the door. This exchange had been a blessing. She'd needed to get away.

It had been only two months since John had left without warning, breaking off their relationship. Before that unforeseen night she'd thought he was the one. Then out of the blue he had announced they were over. His reason being he couldn't compete with her. He'd said she intimidated him.

After that ugly scene she'd decided to put the priority on her career objectives. This trip gave her an opportunity to do just that.

Lucius picked up the bag. Again she waited for him to go first, and he stepped in and placed the luggage on the floor, beside a small sofa that stood in the middle of the room.

Amanda entered slowly, taking in the small but efficient-looking apartment. It consisted of one large room with a beige couch and chair, along with a TV on a stand. A galley kitchen was situated in one corner. She moved further into the room and looked through a door to find the bedroom. The space would be all she needed during her stay.

"I wondered what kind of place the board would put someone up in," Lucius murmured. "I'll have to admit this is about what I expected."

"I'll be comfortable here. I don't have much more than this in Atlanta." Amanda walked to the kitchen counter and put her purse down. "I'm hoping to spend more time at the clinic than I do here anyway. Thanks for bringing up my case. If I'd had to carry it up, I'd be out of breath. By the way, I'm looking forward to working with you at the clinic."

He extended his hand. "It's been nice to meet you."

She placed her hand in his. A jolt of awareness spurred a quick withdrawal. The second Amanda did so she missed the size, heat and strength of his hold.

"I'm…uh…as I said, I look forward to working with you. I've heard some amazing things about you."

He grinned. "I hope you don't believe *all* my press."

"I imagine at least some of it is true."

Amanda walked toward the door. She needed him to leave so she could reorder her nerves, rattled by their brief contact.

"Thank you again."

"Goodbye, Ms…"

"Longstreet."

"Ms. Longstreet. I hope you enjoy your stay in Sydney."

He closed the door behind him as he left.

For some odd reason it seemed as if all the electricity had left the room with him. Shaking off that odd notion, Amanda carried her luggage into the bedroom. There she found a double bed and a nightstand. Off to the left was a door that led to a small bath.

She left the bag near the bed and returned to

the living area. Putting away her clothes could wait. She needed to find a place to buy some food and then she could tend to some other things. After that she'd get a shower and some sleep. Tomorrow would be a big day at the clinic.

Would she see Lucius?

That didn't matter. She wasn't here to dissect and admire Dr. West. Even if he *was* droolworthy, with his fathomless eyes, sexy grin and square jaw.

Kirri had told Amanda he was brilliant, and everything Amanda had read about him confirmed that. However, Lucius West in person was larger than life.

Enough of that kind of thinking. She needed to get busy.

Seeing a notebook on the kitchen counter, she opened it. Inside she found typed details of places to eat, the closest grocery store, laundry, and drug store, along with general information about the area. She was grateful for it.

Now that she was actually here, in the apartment, she felt more invigorated than when she had first stepped off the airplane. All she'd wanted to do then had been to sleep. After her nap—on Lucius, no less—she wanted to do a little exploring and see if she could pick up some food.

Who knew when she would have another chance? There was no telling what the week ahead might bring. She at least needed to buy breakfast items.

All her life she'd been a Girl Scout type of person. Always prepared. In fact, she was known for it. Many a friend in college had turned to her because they knew she'd have what they needed.

Once her roommate had asked to borrow a stapler. Amanda had directed her to the middle desk drawer, in the back, on the left-hand side.

Her roommate's response after she had located the stapler had been, "How do you *do* that?"

Amanda had answered, "I always put things back where they belong."

That part of her personality hadn't endeared her to her stepfather. Despite her being so prepared, and planning things down to the detail, he hadn't accepted her. No matter what she'd done or how good she had been it had never been enough for him. Yet she was loved by the rest of her family.

After washing her face and brushing her hair, she slipped on a clean set of clothes and put on a pair of sunglasses. She needed to stay up for a little while to get acclimated to the time-change. To help with that she decided to walk around the neighborhood in search of the store she'd read about in the notebook.

Heading outside, she turned west along a tree-lined sidewalk. After a few missteps she soon found the small grocery store, not far down the street. She smiled at the girl behind the counter and went down the first aisle.

Picking up a couple of boxes of macaroni and cheese she could use in an emergency, she added a few more items that she could pop into the microwave. She would have liked to buy a gallon of milk, but that would have been too heavy to carry back with all the other stuff she'd gathered.

If she continued to do this type of shopping she would definitely need a rolling bag to make the transportation easier… And if she wanted a wider choice, like fresh produce, she would have to either rent a car or hire a taxi and go to a larger supermarket.

The thought of renting a car came and went. Her trying to drive in town on the opposite side of the road would be more nerve-racking than beneficial especially when she wasn't familiar with the streets. She'd maybe ask someone to drive her when she became acquainted with more people.

She did know one person. *Yeah, right*. Like she would ask Lucius West to drive her around while she shopped. *That* wasn't going to happen.

With both hands full of heavily loaded plastic bags, Amanda left the store and trudged back to the apartment. She had to admit she might have over-bought, but still she had little choice but to keep walking. Not soon enough for her, she arrived.

Setting the bags on the floor, she collapsed on

the couch. She wouldn't have considered herself out of shape, but after such a long plane ride, and not having rested properly, she'd overdone it by going to the store. She'd learned her lesson.

On autopilot she put the cold groceries away, leaving the others until later. With that done, she took a hot shower and climbed into bed.

Her eyelids lowered. The bed was comfortable enough, but somehow the memory of Lucius's shoulder seemed just as nice.

CHAPTER TWO

THREE MORNINGS LATER, as Lucius walked down the hallway toward the procedure room, he thought of Amanda Longstreet. She'd been interrupting his thoughts more often than he wanted to admit. Somehow she had made an indelible impression on him during their brief encounter. But right now he needed to concentrate on his patient. This woman had been trying to have a baby for three years. Nothing so far had proved successful.

As an infertility doctor, he considered hers the type of case he lived for. As a human being, it tore at his heart. He only ever saw women who were desperate for a baby. They either had trouble conceiving or carrying a baby to term. Whichever, his encounters with them invariably included high emotions.

Because of that he always went in and spoke to his patients, instead of just showing up to do the procedure. They were often nervous and fearful, which might contribute to whether or not the in vitro procedure was successful. The calmer and more confident the woman could be, the better the chance of conception.

Entering the room, where his patient waited on the procedure bed, he walked toward her with a sincere smile and hopefully warm assurance. He noticed his nurse, Lucy, was laying out instruments. Another person standing nearby caught his eye. His smile faded a little as he did a double-take.

Amanda.

She grinned and he nodded.

What was she doing here?

He understood she was a Labor and Delivery nurse. Surely that was where she should be. His role was getting women pregnant. It was what he excelled at, although he always had a hard time figuring out how to describe what he specialized in. Usually he defaulted to a very clinical definition.

He raised his chin and nodded to his nurse, then concentrated on his patient.

When he reached Nancy Davis, the prospective mother-to-be, he placed his hand over hers for a moment. "How're you doing?"

"I'm fine. Just a little nervous is all."

He quickly shook hands with her husband, who stood meekly in the corner.

The woman added with a desperate undertone, "This *has* to work."

"I understand. I know you've been through this a couple of times before, but you don't need to worry. I'll be doing all the work here, and I'm going to try something a little innovative during this procedure. I think it will make a difference. I've had success in the lab with it, and that gives me reason to be optimistic. We're not only going to *hope* this takes—we're going to *believe* it will."

She offered him a weak smile. "I sure hope so, Dr. West."

He did too. "You've taken your medication?"

"Yes. But I really need…" She gave a soft sob.

He didn't doubt her need. Even for him, forty thousand dollars or more each time to try and have a baby was a lot of money. It could even grow into more if there were complications. Like multiple babies…

"We'll get started here in a moment. I'm just going out to wash up and then we'll be ready to go."

He left, and soon returned to find Lucy prepared to proceed. Amanda stood beside the patient, near the end of the table, so they could easily see each other. The two women were talking quietly. Nancy's face was expressive as Amanda spoke.

Lucius approached just as Nancy laughed softly. Apparently Amanda had said something funny. The unease he'd seen on his patient's face earlier had disappeared.

He appreciated what Amanda had done. It was crucially important to this procedure that the patient was relaxed. For some unexplained reason it seemed women were often more likely to conceive when they stopped fixating on becoming pregnant. When they just let go. Amanda was helping with that part of the transfer.

He pulled his rolling chair out, settled on it, and moved to Nancy's feet. "I'll be telling you what's happening every step of the way." He moved closer. "Let me know if you feel any discomfort."

"Okay." Nancy's answer was weak, unsure.

"This shouldn't take more than a few minutes. Then we'll let you sit for a while."

The patient's husband moved closer and took Nancy's hand.

"Just like last time?" Nancy asked.

"Yes."

Lucius removed the long flexible tube that held the embryos from the incubator Lucy had rolled to his side. He literally held this couple's hopes in his hand. If all went well, they would soon have a baby.

"Now, this may feel a little different from last time. The embryos aren't at body temperature yet. I want your body to warm them to your own natural temperature."

Amanda's soft gasp caught his attention for a second as she stepped back to stand at his shoulder. Was she planning to interrupt? She made no further move. He returned his full attention to the procedure, forgetting everyone and everything but positioning the embryos in just the correct spot.

Moments later he'd finished, and pushed the stool back so he could see Nancy.

"Now, we're going to let you sit quietly for about thirty minutes. Remember you may have breast tenderness, bloating, cramping, or constipation during the next week or so. I want to see you back in two weeks for your pregnancy test."

"Thank you, Dr. West." Nancy looked at her husband and gave him a hopeful smile.

Lucius headed out the door. In the process of removing his gloves and gown he looked back as the door opened. Amanda entered.

"Nurse Longstreet."

"Hello again, Dr. West." Her words were almost as cool as his.

"How're you adjusting to the clinic?"

"Fine. I've met a lot of great people here." She followed him in the removal of her sterile clothing.

"I'm glad to hear it."

Done, he started out the other door of the room.

"Can I have a minute of your time?" she asked suddenly. "I have a couple of questions about the procedure."

"Oh. Like…?" Something about her tone made him think it might be less curiosity and more concern—or, worse, censure.

"I understand it's not protocol to put embryos in until they're at body temperature, so I was wondering exactly why you felt the need to do it?"

His eyes narrowed and his jaw tightened. He wasn't used to hearing that tone in relation to his work. "And you know about this protocol how…?"

"I've spent the last few days reading your clinic handbook."

Oh. That wasn't the answer he'd expected. "I see you are thorough."

"I try to be." She continued to look at him, as if waiting for an answer to her question.

Lucius shoulders stiffened as he stood straighter. His staff didn't ever question his methods or motives. He was considered by most to be ingenious and successful and his staff followed his lead.

"Do you have concerns about my technique?"

"I'm not exactly concerned about it. It's more like I'm wanting to understand why you did it that way. What if the embryos don't take because of the temperature? Couples invest too much of their life savings, time and emotion in trying to have a baby for you to go rogue. To do something on a hunch."

"Hunch!" He stepped toward her, outraged. "I'll have you know that I've been doing this type of procedure for a long time. There is experience and knowledge behind everything I do. I don't do *hunches.* Couples come to me for one reason and one reason only. They want a baby and I can often make that happen for them."

Amanda's eyes were heated as she glared at

him. "I don't mean to hurt your feelings. I'm asking so I can better understand your thought process."

"That wasn't how it sounded to me. It sounded more like you were questioning my ability and my judgement."

"I'm here to learn about the procedures here from conception to delivery. That's all I'm trying to do."

"I appreciate that, but if you're going to question my skills the entire time you're here then this exchange may not work."

He ran this clinic and he wouldn't have anyone—especially an invited guest—questioning his ethics.

"I'm sorry if I've offended you. And I understand your position, Doctor, but that doesn't mean I'm not supposed to learn and gain knowledge. Part of that's asking questions. I can't learn anything from this exchange if I'm not allowed to ask questions."

"Oh, you're allowed to ask questions. What you're *not* allowed to do is question or react to something I say or do in front of a patient. You are also not allowed to imply, via your questioning, that I might have done something wrong."

Ms. Longstreet certainly had gall.

"So the great 'Baby Whisperer'—" she used sarcastic air quotes with her fingers, which made him grind his back teeth "—doesn't have to explain himself regarding following protocol, or answer to anyone when he has done something outside of the norm. Is that what I'm to understand?"

Lucius shifted from mildly irritated to angry. He took a step closer to her and look down his nose. He couldn't help but admire the fact that Amanda didn't move.

"I think you've hit the nail on the head. Isn't that what they say?"

Amanda straightened to her not inconsiderable height, but still only reached to his shoulders, and took a step toward him. Her nose was now an inch or two from his.

"I'm sorry, Doctor, but where I come from the nurses and the doctors are partners. We're all working toward the same result. We get to question what's being done because it's in our patients' best interest. Our doctors' egos have to take a back seat to that."

His lips thinned into a fine line as he glared at her. How dared she imply that he had less than the best interests for his patients in mind?

"I can assure you that my patients *always* come first."

"I appreciate that. So why do you mind being questioned about how you do something?"

His ire eased a little. "Maybe it's the way you asked me. The tone."

"I didn't realize I had applied any 'tone.'"

She appeared innocent. Lucius stepped back. "I think this conversation has become unproductive. I have work to do."

He left the scrub room and headed down the hallway toward his office. How dared Amanda come into his procedure room for the first time and start interrogating him? Just who did she think she was?

Lucius shook his head. Far more baffling was the fact that he was impressed she had.

An hour later Lucius was still dwelling on his heated conversation with Amanda. Maybe he'd been too rough on her. But Amanda's questions had reminded him too much of his father. He'd always pushed Lucius to explain his decisions, and had questioned his methods so often Lucius had often ended up second-guessing himself.

With his father now in a care home it had been a long time since that had happened. He'd thought he'd outgrown his reaction to having his authority examined. But clearly one small American woman was all it took to bring his youthful insecurities straight back to the surface. He found it infuriating to have his ego on the carpet.

Doctors who did his type of work had to have a strong sense of self-worth—otherwise they would give up. Too often disappointments outweighed celebrations. He lived for the uplifting and exciting times when a woman became pregnant. He needed those to fortify himself against the times when he had to tell a couple the process had failed. He'd seen the pain and the agony too many times. He thoroughly enjoyed the days he attended the Labor and Delivery Room, to see a couple holding a baby after clinging to that dream for so long. Because of those moments he hated to have his efforts second-guessed.

At one time he'd planned to have children of his own when he married, but he had been young and had thought he had plenty of time. The clinic had just opened and it was doing amazing things with great outcomes. He'd nurtured his work, thinking his wife was happy. Instead she had become steadily disgruntled with his long hours.

Melanie had been left to herself too much.

He'd known she enjoyed the social side of being a doctor's wife, and the perks of being married to a rising star in infertility medicine. He'd believed she'd be satisfied with that for a while, but he'd misjudged the depth of her loneliness.

Even when he'd realized he still hadn't been able to tear himself away from the clinic. And when he'd finally tried to make it work, to make changes in his schedule, her answer had been a firm no. Melanie's parting remark had been that he seemed a lot more interested in giving other people babies then he was in having his own.

That hadn't been true. And yet he hadn't felt Melanie's loss like he should have. He'd decided maybe she was right. He was more married to the clinic than to her. After she'd left, he'd seen a few women on and off, but had never let a relationship get past casual. He'd made his mistake and learned from it. He wouldn't try that again.

There hadn't been enough time then and nor was there now to give to a wife and family. There wasn't time for the attention they deserved. He would need somebody who understood the importance of his work and who didn't demand to have his attention on her full-time. That would be a rare person, indeed. One he didn't have time to search for.

Amanda remained perplexed about what had gone wrong between her and Lucius. She'd had no idea asking questions would overstep any professional boundary down here. But she was used to protocol being closely followed and she'd only wanted to know why he hadn't stuck to the usual script.

She had been willing to give him the benefit of the doubt. All she'd wanted was to understand the logic behind his decisions.

But apparently she'd overstepped his boundaries in general—personal as well as professional.

She'd done it again. Another man was feeling challenged by her. *Intimidated.* Some of the men she had dated had accused her of being too rigid, too controlling. She hadn't been what they wanted. She was too demanding. Time after time with a man, as soon as she'd let her guard down and allowed her true nature to show, he'd found fault with her character. None had been tactful in their criticism.

After the shock and heartache of her last love interest's rejection, she'd put her dream of finding Mr. Right, getting married and starting a family to one side for a while. Instead she'd turned her concentration on her career goals and put all her energy into achieving them.

That had meant coming here to Harborside and being involved in the amazing work Lucius and his staff were doing in reproduction. The experience would be an important stepping-stone to becoming Director of Nursing at her clinic back home.

Somehow she had to neutralize Lucius's animosity and earn his respect. She had to put them back on the footing they'd been on before he'd left her apartment that first night.

She had no doubt he was a gifted and dedicated doctor. But how could she have known that asking forthright questions about his procedural decisions was off-limits? Come to think of it, he'd become annoyed with her far too quickly. Did that unexpected reaction mean she'd called attention to him doing something he shouldn't? Or was he hyper-sensitive for some other reason?

She shook her head to clear the unanswerable questions away. She'd spend her time learning and gaining all the invaluable experience she could while she was here, and stay out of his way as much as possible.

After he'd left her in a huff she'd gone back to the Labor and Delivery Department. There she'd joined one of the nurses she had met on her first day at the clinic.

Apart from Lucius, everyone on the staff had been friendly, and more than willing to answer her questions. If they didn't know the answer off the top of their head, they'd made an effort to find out.

Now, as Amanda strolled toward her apartment, she found herself continuing to be distracted by her confrontation with Lucius.

The clinic was amazing, and doing some outstanding work—it was everything Kirri had said it was. The only issue Amanda had was with Lucius. Her unintentional professional offense had put a damper on her visit. He had been so kind about taking her luggage up to her apartment, proving her first impression of him wrong. And from that she'd assumed they'd gotten past the initial rough spot of getting acquainted.

Yet here they were.

Kirri was such a charming person Amanda hadn't imagined there'd be any issue with her brother. And when Lucius had made the comment about the exchange not working Amanda had been shocked. She didn't appreciate being threatened. She'd actively campaigned to participate in this exchange and she needed to record it on her résumé as being a successful experience. Lucius's subtle implication that he might send her back to Atlanta in disgrace made her feel sick.

She had to figure out some way to work this out…smooth things over with him. After a night's sleep and a good think she'd form a plan to convince him that she'd respect his professional space in future.

Climbing the stairs, she entered her apartment. She'd bought a few things at the local department store to make the space a little more "hers". A vase with a few flowers now sat on the coffee table. She had also found a couple of inexpensive yellow throw pillows to add to the sofa. The items gave the tiny space some personality. She liked living in Sydney. It would be easy to make it like home.

The next morning, she arose determined to speak to Lucius as soon as she could. She'd tossed and turned all night, rehearsing what she would say. Somehow she needed to get him back on her side.

As soon as she had a free moment at the clinic, she went in search of him. After being directed to his office she discovered he wasn't there. She pulled up the procedure schedule to see if he was doing one. He wasn't. She finally found somebody who told her to check the nursery.

Despite being sure she'd heard the nurse correctly, she couldn't imagine why Lucius would be in the baby nursery. But Amanda didn't argue and went to look.

To her great surprise, she *did* find Lucius there, sitting in a rocking chair holding a sleeping newborn.

Amanda's breath caught in her throat. Her heart softened at the sight of the big man holding the small child so tenderly. He looked at ease, like she hadn't seen him before. As if he had no worries in the world or any concerns about this famous clinic and his part in it.

The man before her now and the man she'd known yesterday were two vastly different people. Never would she have guessed that she would see him like this.

It took her a few moments to compose herself. She stood there enthralled, wanting to take in this perfect example of what was right with the world.

A nurse brushed by her and broke the mood.

Amanda took a couple of steps forward. "Dr. West—Lucius?"

He gave her a preoccupied look.

The fleeting thought that he'd make a good father went through her head. She didn't need to have those types of ideas about Lucius. They weren't going to become friendly enough for her to have that kind of opinion about him. Hadn't Kirri said he was married to his job? So much so his marriage had failed?

"Yes, Nurse Longstreet?"

"I…uh… I was wondering if you had a moment so we could talk?"

"I have a procedure in about twenty minutes."

She looked around. Was that a no? She wasn't giving up. "Maybe I could buy you a cup of coffee?"

"I'm sorry, I don't drink it this time of the day."

He wasn't making this easy for her. "A soft drink?"

One of the babies cried. "As you can see, I'm a little busy here. What do you want to discuss?"

She clasped her hands together and took a step toward him. "I'd really appreciate it if we could talk about what happened yesterday."

He looked toward one of the cribs and nodded his head to the side. "Grab that baby and have a seat."

Amanda scooped the newborn into her arms. A nurse entered, saw Amanda, and stepped out again. Amanda took a seat in the rocking chair across from Lucius. Holding the baby close, she rocked and cooed. The child settled.

"I believe you have a knack for handling babies," he said.

The admiration in his voice warmed her in an unexpected way.

"I can do more than deliver them. And I've held more than one in my time. Including a niece and a nephew."

A shadow entered Lucius's eyes and then was quickly gone. Great—she'd said something else to upset him when she had been trying to gain his trust.

Softly she said, "I thought the babies stayed in the room with their mothers."

"Most of them do, but we take in foundlings without question. This is a safe place for mothers to leave their unwanted babies. And one or two babies belong to mothers who had difficult deliveries and need their rest. That's why we have this many in here right now."

The baby Lucius held let out a gentle sigh.

"I see you have some skill in this area too," said Amanda.

"Thanks. This is a good place to come and decompress."

Lucius needed to decompress? He gave the impression he had everything under control at all times.

She looked around to see if the nurse had returned. "Look, Lucius...um... Dr. West, I want to apologize about yesterday. I didn't intend to question your authority. I certainly would never undermine you in front of a patient. I'm sorry if you felt I had."

"I appreciate that. However, after some thought I believe I might have overreacted to what you asked me."

Amanda struggled to conceal her astonishment. She hadn't expected him to say anything like that.

Lucius continued. "I was raised by a man who constantly questioned what I did. Consequently I don't like to be interrogated about my decisions."

For a moment he frowned, as if confused about what he'd said.

When he didn't continue, she offered, "Thank you for sharing that. Now I understand your negative reaction to my professional curiosity. This exchange program is important to me. I need it to go well."

"Why's that?"

Should she reveal something as personal as her hopes and dreams? But her career plans weren't a secret, and she was too far from home for it to matter if she talked about them.

"I believe coming here is my opportunity to get an important promotion back home. The fact that I'm here watching you perform such innovative procedures, and learning how and why you operate as you do, can only be good for my career. As lofty as it sounds, I want to help hurting women have babies."

"In that we'll always agree."

For some reason that gave Amanda a warm feeling—as if they had found solidarity on this particular point, no matter their personal issues.

The nurse stuck her head in the door. "Dr. West, they're ready for you in the procedure room."

"Please tell them I'm on my way."

He slowly rose and gently laid the baby in a bassinet. He looked at Amanda, still holding the now sleeping infant.

"I'll see to it that you get every opportunity to learn while you're here. Including getting answers to any questions you may have."

"Thank you, Lucius. I'd really appreciate that."

He lifted the child from her arms with practiced ease and lay her in the empty crib.

Amanda stood and Lucius extended his hand. "Agreed?"

She slipped her hand into his. An electric volt shot through her, as it had the first time he'd clasped her hand. They shook hands.

Too soon, or perhaps not soon enough, he let her hand go and headed for the door leading to the hall.

"See you around," he threw over his broad shoulder with a sincere smile.

He left her feeling muddled in his wake. One minute he had been angry with her and the next he'd acted with understanding and been agreeable.

And he hadn't reacted to the revelation of her career ambitions as she'd expected. What a challenge he had become to understand.

Still befuddled, she checked the sleeping baby before leaving. She liked challenges. Especially intriguing and handsome ones.

* * *

The next afternoon in Labor and Delivery, Amanda prepared to help deliver a baby. This one was the result of a second IVF transfer. The mother had conceived the first time, but lost the baby in the first trimester.

The parents-to-be were today equally anxious and excited. Just after Amanda had begun working with couples battling infertility she had learned that these primary emotions were part and package of a clinic atmosphere.

Amanda made a quick review of the mother's medical chart on the computer tablet she held. Excitement bubbled within her. This would be the first time she'd helped with a delivery since coming to Harborside.

The birth of a baby was always exhilarating for the parents, but it was an equal thrill for the delivery staff as well. A new human being coming into the world for parents who had gone the extra mile or more to conceive made these babies extra-special. Nothing compared to the joy of this type of delivery.

Amanda slipped into her gown and gloves as the mother settled herself on the delivery table. Dr. Leah Johannsson, whom she had met on her first day at the clinic, would be handling the delivery. She was a small, soft-spoken woman in her mid-forties, with serious brown eyes. Amanda could understand why she was one of the patients' favorites.

Moments later Dr. Johannsson entered, dressed in gown and gloves as well.

The head nurse had told Amanda there was some anxiety about this birth, since the mother had lost one baby before. She had been on bed-rest for the last three months, spending the last two weeks in the clinic's in-care unit. The goal had been to prevent an early birth.

Entering the delivery room, Amanda stepped beside the bed and smiled at the mother. "I'm Amanda Longstreet, a clinical nurse visiting from America. I'm honored to be helping with your de-livery today. I look forward to meeting your baby."

"I look forward to meeting Alease too," the mother answered, smiling her happiness.

"What a beautiful name."

"Thanks. We're naming her after my grand-mother." The woman winced.

"I think Alease is telling us she thinks it's time to meet her parents." Amanda looked over at the man hovering next to his wife, holding her hand.

The woman sucked in a breath as another pain came.

Amanda stepped back, letting Dr. Johannsson move in next to the bed. "I think this is going to happen sooner rather than later," she said.

Another pain gripped the patient.

"On the next one I want you to push," Dr. Johannsson instructed.

Minutes passed, and then the doctor said, "Don't push. I know you want to, but don't."

Seconds filled with heavy tension ticked by before she said, "*Now* it's time to bear down."

Slowly, little Alease slipped into the world.

The mother sighed and giggled at the same time.

Amanda switched her attention from her to the baby. Her heart caught. Something was wrong. The baby was blue. Not breathing. Limp. A pool of red fell to the floor.

Dr. Johannsson said quietly, "I need some help here."

The doctor quickly handed the baby to Amanda. The mother was bleeding and the baby was in trouble.

Amanda rushed to the warmer, on her way hitting the emergency button on the wall that would bring additional help. Placing the baby inside the warmer, she dried her and started giving her stimulation with her fingers at the same time. Removing the wet blanket and dropping it to the floor, she quickly tapped the baby's feet, hoping for a small sound. *Nothing.* She then checked the heartrate, using two fingers under the base of the umbilical cord.

Sensing more than seeing, Amanda became aware that more people had entered the room.

The heart rate-remained below one hundred and the baby still hadn't cried. She opened the baby's airway and reached for an oxygen mask. A large hand was already placing it over the baby's nose and mouth and giving it a pump.

She glanced up to see Lucius.

Still the baby wasn't breathing. Amanda quickly checked the airway. Chest compressions were needed.

"You take over the oxygen."

She didn't wait for Lucius to respond. Wrapping her hands around the baby, with her thumbs under the center of her chest, she pushed.

"On my count," she told Lucius. "*One*, two, three," she recited, like counting for a waltz. "Breathe."

Lucius pumped the oxygen bag.

"*One*, two, three. Breathe."

He stayed with the beat she set. They worked for a minute. Then she stopped chest compressions and checked vitals. The baby moved. Amanda felt as if she could finally breathe herself. Lucius removed the oxygen mask. The baby let out a loud cry.

She smiled at Lucius and he returned it. His smile reached his eyes and caused a quiver in her middle.

"Well done, Amanda." His words were soft, and loaded with appreciation.

She nodded before turning her attention to the

baby, wrapping her in a blanket and gently pulling a knit cap over the now healthy and pink head. Done, she looked to Dr. Johannsson, who was still working with the mom. She checked the baby's vitals again. Lucius still stood nearby, but didn't hover over them.

"Nurse Longstreet," Dr. Johannsson said, "I believe Mommy and Daddy would like to see their new baby girl now."

Grinning, she carried the baby to the mother and laid her on her chest. They would be allowed to bond for a few minutes and then Amanda would take Alease to NICU for evaluation.

A few tender moments later the mother, with tears in her eyes, looked beyond Amanda and said, "Thank you, Dr. West."

Amanda watched him. Lucius hadn't moved from where he stood near the wall.

He nodded. "You're welcome."

Amanda studied him another moment. He appeared nonchalant, but she could see the moisture in his eyes.

When she turned again, having taken the baby from her mother, he was gone.

Well, well, well. That's twice in a week I've caught a glimpse of Dr. Lucius West's tender side.

CHAPTER THREE

LUCIUS WALKED FROM the parking lot toward all the activity in the beach park. The clinic's annual picnic had been planned for today. All the families who had been helped through the clinic were invited. Many came to show off the children they were so proud of. It had become the best professional day of his entire year and was one he always looked forward to. Even the staff members brought their families.

After the picnic meal there would be contests, like the cutest baby, or the best sandcastle, and games and whatever else the picnic committee had come up with. Then the group picture of the children would be taken. That photo would be blown up and framed, then hung in the lobby of the clinic.

There were families everywhere. Adults stood in groups, talking. Some held small babies while others watched children run up and down the nearby beach. Seeing all the children gave him a sense of accomplishment that came along with the knowledge that he had helped create all this happiness. The sight humbled him.

A number of parents came up to him and thanked him. He had to remind more than one couple that he hadn't done it on his own, and that his excellent staff had been involved as well. For him, it was the way he made his living, but for these parents having a child was a dream come true.

It didn't take him long to tire of their adoration. He just wanted to enjoy the sunny, warm day with happy people at the beach. Seldom did he have a chance to do it. His work came first and taking time off for a social event usually fell pretty low on his list of priorities.

He approached the shelter that was located in a grassy area. A long table had been stationed there. Another table had been left out in the open, so people could eat there. Brightly colored table-cloths covered them. The clinic had provided all the food. He saw a caterer overseeing the meat and shrimp on the barbecue. His mouth watered at the wonderful smell coming from that direction.

A few of his staff mingled under the tent. He spied Amanda, talking to a couple of staff members in the corner. She wore a soft yellow dress that left her shoulders bare. The breeze blew her skirt, highlighting her curves. They were nice ones. She laughed. It reminded him of a church bell on a clear Sunday morning. It rippled through him, leaving peace in its wake. This woman had too much of an effect on him for his liking.

A male staff member placed his hand on her shoulder. Amanda smiled at him. Their friendliness disturbed Lucius. She'd never looked at *him* like that. Maybe he hadn't given her reason to. But that wasn't an area he intended to explore. After all, his days of caring if a woman smiled at him or not were long gone. His work gave him all the emotional satisfaction he needed in his life.

Besides, Amanda was a visiting professional from America. She wouldn't be here for very long and he wasn't interested in a fling, however brief. Even if he was it wouldn't be with someone working at the clinic. When an intimate relationship in the workplace ended it caused too much drama and damage, making the workplace uncomfortable.

If he ever seriously considered becoming involved with a woman again, he knew their time together would be easy, casual and short. He'd always made it clear to the women he dated that he wasn't interested in perpetuating any "true love" fantasy with them.

He could well understand why men found Amanda interesting. He did. There was nothing more magnetic than a woman who knew who she was and what she wanted. Something about Amanda made him think that was just the case with her. She wasn't the type to depend on a man to make her feel confident. She seemed strong in her own right, could stand on her own two feet, and would dare anyone to say she couldn't. He really liked that about her.

His ex-wife had relied on *him* for her identity. Then one day she hadn't. He hadn't been able too support both her emotional neediness and his commitments at the clinic.

Someone called his name and he turned. Amanda's gaze met his. A primal awareness zipped through him. She smiled, leaving the group she'd been talking to and coming over to join him.

"I'm surprised to see you here. I didn't think this type of event would be your sort of thing," she remarked.

"Where d'you get that idea?"

"Kirri, possibly. She implied you're not very sociable. Maybe just a little bit rigid."

Amanda said it as if she agreed with his sister. Just how much had Kirri talked about him to her?

"Do you always just say whatever comes to your mind?" he asked. "And by the way I'm perfectly sociable." He raised his chin. "When I want to be."

She grinned. "Well, that's nice to know. And, yes, I do always say what I think. How else am I supposed to learn things?"

"And today you've learned what, exactly?"

"That you're sociable despite your unsociable expression." Her smile turned cheeky. "You *can* smile, Doctor. No one will think any less of you."

The woman exasperated him, but he couldn't stop the lift of his lips. "Just so you know, this happens to be my favorite event of the year. It's nice to see how the babies have grown…become children."

Amanda looked at all the teeming activity around them. Her gaze settled on him again. Somehow having her sole attention made him feel special.

"You must be very proud. You certainly have the right to be."

"I'll admit it's nice to see all the families I've helped create. But enough talk about that." He looked at her. "Does the Atlanta clinic have this sort of event?"

"No, but I'm going to recommend they do. It's a wonderful PR opportunity. Plus, it gives the staff a chance to appreciate their good work. Not to mention it's loads of fun."

"Hey, Lucius!" Nancy, his nurse, called to him as she entered the tent. "I'm glad you came."

"I wouldn't miss it." He grinned.

"We're about ready to start serving. You want to say something before we do?" Nancy asked.

"Why don't you do it?" said Lucius. He would rather just remain part of the crowd.

Nancy dared to tug his forearm. "You know they want to hear from *you*. You could at least welcome them."

He glanced at Amanda, who still smiled even while giving him an expectant look, as if she would be disappointed if he didn't do as Nancy requested.

"Okay."

A few minutes later Nancy had seen to it that everyone had gathered close. Lucius proceeded to tell everyone how thankful he was to have them there and say he hoped they enjoyed their day.

Nancy stepped up as he finished. "We need to get the group picture of the children, then we'll eat."

Lucius moved away, sliding off to the side.

"Very inspirational speech, Dr. West."

He recognized Amanda's voice. She stood at his elbow, watching him with unnerving intensity.

"It was more short and sweet than inspirational," he replied.

"You really don't like the limelight, do you?" she asked.

"Not really. You ready to eat?" To his surprise, he found he wanted to talk to her about something other than work.

"Starving."

"Then come on and—let's get something off the barbie before it's all gone." He led her to where the paper plates were stacked and they began filling theirs.

Amanda turned to him. "Do you have someone you're supposed to eat with?"

"No. I was hoping you'd let me join you."

What was he doing? That sounded like he was singling her out. Was he sure he wanted to do that? Yeah, he did. He had become tired of his own company. Amanda made him think, and question his answers. Her wit kept him on his toes. A feat few people could accomplish. What harm would there be in getting to know her better?

"That's my towel over there." She pointed it out on the beach. "The one that looks like the Australian flag."

"Why am I not surprised?"

She grinned. "I bought it yesterday afternoon, knowing I'd need one today. It'll make a good souvenir of my time here in Australia."

He rolled his eyes. Even *he* didn't own anything that patriotic. "I'm sure it will."

"If you'll take my plate, I'll go get us some drinks. What would you like?"

"A soft drink will be fine."

"I'll be there in a sec. Don't eat my food." Amanda left him with a smile on her face.

What he found amazing was the fact that he had one on his face as well. He didn't make a habit of smiling like a silly schoolboy with a crush on the pretty new teacher, but Amanda brought that out in him. Much to his dismay, he was finding everything about her was exhilarating.

Nancy and a couple more staff members joined them, after spreading their own towels and blankets nearby. In one way he was glad to have the distraction from Amanda, but in another he knew he would miss having her undivided attention.

"Amanda," Nancy said, "you've been here a week—tell us what you think about Australia? The clinic? Where you're living?"

"I'm lovin' Australia. Everybody's been so kind."

She glanced at him. Her eyes twinkled. Was she reminding him that all hadn't been smooth between them? That maybe he'd been the exception?

"I really like working at the clinic. Y'all have an exceptional program."

Lucius loved Amanda's drawled out "y'all". Did her accent become stronger when she was aroused? He'd really like to find out...

Lucius choked on his drink.

Everyone focused on him. Amanda studied him with concern. He gave a quick cough to clear his throat.

Amanda continued, "My apartment is nice. I've found a place close by to go for groceries, and a department store for other things about five blocks away. The only thing I'm sad about is that I haven't had a chance yet to see much of the city. I'm planning to do some sightseeing tomorrow. Be a real tourist. I want to see the Sydney Harbor Bridge—from the top—the Opera House at least from the outside, and then maybe go to the zoo. I can't go home without seeing a koala. They're *so* cute."

She sounded like a little girl talking about her

favorite doll at Christmas. He found it fascinating that the same woman who went about her job so efficiently and systematically was chatting about sightseeing like an excited child. Who was the real Amanda and why did she fill him with awe every time she was near him?

"You need to visit one of the smaller zoos where you can hold one," one of the staff members said.

Amanda leaned forward. Her eyes wide and bright. "You can do that? Really?"

A male staff member nodded. "Sure. There's a place a few hours out of town where you can. Just take the train."

"I'm gonna have to look that up. Maybe I can go next weekend. Thanks for letting me know. Oh, one more thing. I plan to take a ferry ride across the harbor. See Sydney by water. For us landlocked people in Atlanta, living around this much water is incredible." She paused, looking off toward the ocean. "I might do that this afternoon."

On the tip of Lucius's tongue were the words, *I could show you around*, but he stopped himself saying them by stuffing food in his mouth.

"Have you been to The Strand?" Nancy asked.

"What's that?"

"It's a huge Victorian building full of shops. The building alone is worth seeing. But the shopping is great too."

Lucius groaned, along with a couple of the other males.

Amanda looked at each of them with annoyance, before giving Lucius a pointed glare. "Not *everyone* thinks about work all the time."

Silence fell over the group. Amanda's confusion was plain. His staff would be shocked to hear her speak to him that way. Few people joked with him, or called him out on how he spent his time. That would be no one except his sister, but up until recently she hadn't had much room to talk either.

To get the conversation back on track, Lucius said, "I think it's a beautiful building as well. The stained glass is remarkable on a sunny day."

Amanda relaxed as the others' unease disappeared. But he knew they continued to watch his interaction with Amanda with interest.

He shifted so he could see her more clearly. "You do know there are other things to do around the city that aren't so touristy?"

Amanda straightened, as if his question had been intended to scold her. "Like what?"

He shrugged. "Like going to one of the public ocean pools. They're built right on the ocean. Filled with ocean water. It's an amazing experience to swim in one in the early morning and watch the day come alive."

The others stared at him as if they suddenly had no idea who he was.

"That sounds lovely."

Amanda's voice had turned breathy. It stirred him in ways and places that hadn't been moved in a long time.

"I'm gonna have to do that," she said.

"I'll tell you what—I'll pick you up next Saturday and we'll go for a swim."

He glanced at the others. Their eyes had grown wide and their mouths had become slack. He'd shocked them.

Thankfully one of the staff members down the beach called out, "The games start in fifteen minutes! So finish up your food but leave room for ice cream."

Their little group returned to eating, but occasionally he noticed one or more of them watching him with a smile. Nancy clearly wore a smirk. Thankfully, Amanda seemed oblivious to any undercurrents.

Minutes before they were called to the first game everyone dispersed, leaving him and Amanda alone. He stood and offered his hand to help her up. She studied it for a second and then put her fingers in his. As soon as she got to her feet he released her hand. They placed their trash in a can and walked toward the crowd that was forming.

"I have to oversee the Pie-in-the-Face game," she said. "And I'm still looking for someone to be the face." She gave him a pointed look.

He had no plans to compete in any of the games. He didn't do games. He couldn't think of anything worse than waiting to have whipped cream repeatedly thrown in his face.

Amanda stopped walking and he did too. She continued to look at him. "Will you do it?" she asked. "I think the parents as well as the kids would love it. I know the staff would too."

His eyes narrowed. "What do you mean by that?"

She lifted a shoulder and dropped it. "I believe they think you're a bit of a stuffed shirt. But I know better."

He took off his sunglasses and leaned down so he could see her eyes clearly. "And how do you know that?"

"Because I've seen you in the nursery. You're really a softy under all the bark and gruff."

Lucius threw back his head and laughed. "Ms. Longstreet, I've never met another woman like you."

She smiled. "Is that a good thing or a bad thing?"

"To tell you the truth, I'm not sure yet. But I think today I'd like to prove to my staff how *un-*stuffed my shirt really is."

Amanda's smile grew to a satisfied grin. "I knew you'd do it."

He slipped his glasses back into place. "So sure of yourself, are you?"

Her nose went in the air. "I got you to do something that Nancy said would never happen."

He'd been had. Manipulated. And the worst thing about it was that for some reason he didn't mind at all...

They joined the crowd and for the next hour watched the games. Amanda really got into them. She laughed, clapped and cheered. How animated she became was something to behold. He noticed how many of the staff spoke to her as they passed, or stood next to her in the crowd. She was popular.

Too soon for him, she said, "It's time to get you ready."

They walked over to where a clown doctor had been painted on a board. The face had been cut out.

"We need to get you dressed." Amanda stepped behind the board.

"Dressed?" he asked.

She nodded and reached into a cloth bag on the ground. "Yeah. You'll want to put on a plastic bag to cover your clothes. Come around here." She waved him toward her.

He gave her a dubious look. "You've done this before, haven't you?"

"I have. This was my idea." She shook out a large trash bag and pulled a hole in the end.

"So this was planned for me all along?"

She shrugged. "Raise your arms."

Lucius did as she said. She stood on her toes and reached up to slip the bag over his head. He leaned forward and emerged to find them almost face to face. Amanda stood so close he could clearly smell her over the ocean. Her scent reminded him of the roses his gardener had grown in his back yard. Their gazes met. She had flakes of gold in her beautiful eyes. He could just make out a few freckles over the bridge of her nose.

He leaned forward, then stopped himself. This wasn't the time or the place to kiss her. But he badly wanted to. Instead he met her gaze. "You do know I'm going to get you for this?"

A mischievous grin formed on her lips. "Is that a promise, Dr. West?"

He stepped forward, sandwiching her between himself and the back of the board. Her look dared him. Time ticked by as the air between them became hot and heavy.

"It certainly is," he said at last.

She licked her lips, sending blood straight to his manhood.

"I expect promises to be kept."

The sound of people approaching made him quickly step back. What was he *doing*? He had better sense than to flirt with Amanda—especially in public. But it was so much fun. It had been a long time since he'd felt this alive.

"Let me fix some holes for your arms." She

moved to his side and tore another hole in the trash bag. He pushed his hand through.

"I can do the other one." His voice sounded gruffer than he'd intended.

"Okay. I'm going around to the other side and take care of the cream pies. You just stick your face through the hole." She started around the board, then stopped and gave him a wicked grin. "And smile."

Lucius did as she instructed. He looked out at the faces standing before him. Children of every size waited in a line with eager looks on their faces. A small table had been set up nearby. Pie pans filled with white, fluffy whipped cream sat in lines on it. Nancy was working at adding cream from a can to even more pans.

Amanda handed a child of about eight one of the plates. "Now, give it a big throw."

The pie came through the air with cream flying around it, straight toward him. To Lucius's great relief it hit the bottom of the board. He grinned. "Maybe next time."

Another child took his place. His pie hit just to the right side of Lucius's face. This was starting to be fun. Children kept coming. They continued to miss. All he had on his face were a few dollops of cream.

"Since we all seem to be missing Dr. West, we're going to move the throwing line a little closer for the second round," Amanda announced.

The crowd roared and clapped. Lucius growled and glared at Amanda. She just smiled sweetly at him.

The first few children missed again. Then one finally hit the side of his face. The next two managed to get him in the forehead. The next throw hit him square-on. The crowd went wild with laugher and hollering. Before the line was finished his face had been completely covered in cream. He had to blink to keep it out of his eyes.

Not soon enough for him, Amanda announced, "I think Dr. West deserves a hand for being such a good sport."

A big cheer rose to join the applause.

Nancy stepped between him and the crowd. "Thanks for coming to this year's picnic, everyone. See you next year."

Lucius pulled his face back from the hole and started wiping it clean with his hand. Amanda joined him behind the board with a bag in her hand.

He grumbled, "I can't believe I let you talk me into doing that."

She giggled. "You looked so shocked when that first pie hit you in the face."

"It's not funny."

"Yeah, it is."

"I'll show you how funny it is."

He grabbed her and rubbed his cheek against hers, then ran it over her forehead, leaving a large smear of cream. He stopped only long enough to turn his head and do it again. All the time she squealed and squirmed, making the mess greater. With one last pass he scrubbed his nose along hers. Then he suddenly stopped. Looking at her mouth, he licked some cream from the corner and brought his tongue in, tasting the sweet mixture of cream and Amanda.

She stilled. Her look of wonder remained fixed on him.

His gaze met hers. "You taste good," he said.

She ran her finger across his jaw, collecting some more cream. Her eyes glinted suggestively. She stuck it in her mouth and then pulled it out slowly.

Hot blood rushed to below his belt. This thing between them had taken on a life of its own here in broad daylight, on a public beach, in front of his staff. Where children might see.

Not the time or the place. Once again.

He backed away.

Amanda blinked. The mesmerizing sparkle in her eyes disappeared. She reached for her bag and pulled out a roll of paper towels. Pulling some off, she handed them to him. He wiped his face clean, then began pulling the plastic bag over his head.

"Here, let me help you," Amanda said. Seconds later the bag was gone. "You missed a spot. Let me get it for you."

"No."

If she touched him again there would definitely be a show to see.

He lowered his voice. "That's all right. I'm going home after this. I'll clean up there."

Confusion and hurt filled her eyes. "Okay. Thanks for helping out today. You were quite a hit. The kids and parents loved it. And once again you proved you have a soft heart."

"Soft heart?"

"You say that like you think it's a bad thing. I think it makes you very special."

He whipped his head toward her.

She continued cleaning up, not meeting his look.

"I'm sorry I shouldn't have said that. Your secret is safe with me. You're free to go. Thanks for your help," she added.

"Not a problem."

As he walked away the temptation to ask if she needed a ride home crossed his mind—but did he really want to get involved with Amanda? *No.* And she couldn't really be interested in him either, could she? They lived on two different continents, in different worlds. Right now they worked together, and he had rules. All that could happen between them was a brief, meaningless fling.

He suspected she was the type of woman who wouldn't go for that. Something about Amanda made him think she'd want forever. But he'd traveled that road once and it had ended in a wreck.

That wasn't a place he intended to revisit. Nothing but sexual electricity could exist between him and Amanda.

Still, it was hot…and enticing. He still carried the scorch of her touch and the wicked thoughts that had come with her licking that whipped cream off her finger. But acting on those desires would be at best a distraction, at worst possible destruction. He was much better off walking away.

Lucius made it to his car and drove home with the distinct sensation that he was running from something dangerous and desirable, and that he should be scared.

Amanda stood trembling as her blood surged through her. What had she been *thinking* to tease Lucius like that? To act so suggestively and then make such a statement about his personality. Had she lost her mind? She hadn't been thinking or she wouldn't have done it. Now he probably thought she'd been coming on to him.

Ugh.

For a second there she'd been afraid he might kiss her. Worse, she had no doubt she would have let him. That would have been a ten on a scale of one to ten in *wrong*. She hadn't come halfway around the world to start kissing the head of the Harborside clinic. Her future depended on her being totally professional. She certainly didn't want it to get out that she'd been coming on to the boss. All thought of ever doing so stopped here. *Now.*

She held out her shaking hand. Her body wasn't listening.

She finished gathering the trash with renewed determination. The crowd had thinned, and everyone was making their way to the parking lot. She needed to go home and regroup. Forget about Lucius West and his sexy blue eyes that saw too much, watched her too closely. Becoming involved with Lucius would be a grave mistake—both professionally and personally. She needed to step back, re-evaluate what she should do.

Placing her palm to her forehead, she groaned. She'd agreed to go swimming with him next Saturday morning. *Not* a good plan.

Twenty-four hours later she was still mentally bemoaning her attraction to Lucius as she explored the city. She'd spent some time outside the Opera House, studying its amazing architecture. From there she'd found her way to the Harbor Bridge. Now she was climbing it.

A few times she wanted to stop, but she knew it was further to go back down than it was to continue climbing up. Proud of herself for making it to the top, she stood looking out at the beautiful view.

She could only imagine what it would be like to see this scene every day. She wished she had someone to share it with. Lucius came to mind, but she quickly pushed his face away.

Too tired to do more, she returned to her apartment. The ferry ride on the harbor would have to wait for another day. She had several more weekends before she left for home.

By the end of the next day, Sunday, she'd decided that avoiding Lucius during the next week would the answer to getting out of going swimming with him, and even more importantly would help her avoid any chance of furthering the attraction she felt for him.

Maybe he'd even forget about his offer. Except for that one suggestive moment at the beach, he hadn't acted as if he wanted any more to do with her. In fact, he'd almost run away from her. Whatever those moments had been between them Lucius obviously didn't want any further involvement. Or maybe he feared her for some reason. She couldn't make out what his response meant.

She'd give him an out on his invitation by just not being around. She'd stay close to Labor and Delivery and out of his path. Although she wasn't sure she *wanted* him to forget about it. As contrary as he was, she liked him.

Amanda knew she could always decline his invitation. Say that she had changed her mind. But she really wanted to go. Not only to see the pool but to spend time with Lucius. The only thing keeping her from acting on her attraction was her fear of liking him *too* much. Surely they could just be friends without indulging in their sexual attraction?

She would never have thought the self-important guy who had climbed into the car with her that first day would ever appeal to her. But the Lucius who held babies just to decompress, or the Lucius who had shown up at the beach party she could like—a lot. She'd only known him a week and his merest touch made her body tingle with possibilities.

But she must be careful. More than one man had shown interest in her and then let her down. With Lucius she couldn't afford to make any mistakes. It would matter not only emotionally but career-wise as well. Teasing was one thing—kissing was another.

To her amazement, she made it almost to the end of the week without ever seeing Lucius. But by Thursday afternoon she had Lucius withdrawal symptoms. She even stooped to searching out when he was in the lab or doing a procedure. She learned that he hadn't even been at the clinic because he'd been out of town.

Even so, more than once she nervously looked up, expecting to see him while she worked on helping deliver a baby, because one of the nurses had mentioned he might attend this birth.

All this avoidance kept her on a tightrope of

stress. She wasn't sure how much longer she could keep it up.

"Amanda? Dr. West called down and he would like for you to go to his office," one of the nurses announced suddenly.

"Right now?"

Amanda's heart did a flip. *Lucius wanted to see her.* As far as she could tell up till now he'd been avoiding her as well.

She looked down to find her hands shaking. "Please let him know I'm with a patient right now and will be there as soon as I can."

Amanda returned to checking the woman's vitals, thankful she could do it by rote since her mind had gone elsewhere.

Finally finished with the patient, she addressed the other nurse. "I'm off to see Dr. West. Let me know if you need me to come back."

"If there's a problem I'll page you. Don't look so scared." The nurse grinned.

Amanda returned a thin-lipped smile. "I just wish I knew what this was about."

"I've never heard of him biting anyone."

"There's always a first time."

Lucius could nibble on her anytime, she thought, but she was sure that wasn't what he wanted to see her about. Even if she would have enjoyed it.

Making her way to Lucius's office, she walked into the business section of the building. No one sat behind the reception desk. She went to knock on what she thought might be Lucius's office door, but hesitated.

Before she could knock a woman she had been introduced to at the picnic came to the desk.

"Are you looking for Dr. West?" she asked.

"Yes. I was told he wanted to see me."

"You'll find him in the lab. It's hard to tie him to his chair long enough to do any type of paperwork. He loves that lab."

Amanda wasn't surprised.

"It's down the hall." The middle-aged woman pointed. "Turn left and it's the third door on the left."

Amanda followed her directions with trepidation and anticipation. She had no idea what to expect. Her reaction to Lucius reminded her of being next to a fire, feeling toasty and warm but knowing if she stepped too close she could get burnt.

She entered the door marked "Lab." Inside there was a glass wall, and a door made out of the same material. She could see Lucius. He was wearing a white lab coat, seated on a stool, with a large syringe in his hand as he worked on a rack of test tubes.

He looked up when she knocked on the glass. Their gazes met. She'd forgotten what a powerful effect he had on her. A wave of sexual awareness hit her midsection. She stood motionless for a moment.

With a gesture of his hand, he indicated for her to come in, but pointed toward the right. She looked in that direction and found a dressing room. After a nod, she gowned up. Done, she entered through the glass door. It made a swishing sound as the airlock sealed.

For a second, she smiled. She and Lucius were locked in together.

"You wanted to see me?" she said.

He turned toward her. His vivid eyes gave her a searching look. He seemed satisfied with what he saw.

"Yes. I thought you might be interested in something I'm working on. You said you wanted to know about the process from start to finish. Since I'm working in the lab today, I thought it would be a good time to show you."

Her concern at being in his presence quickly became overridden by her eagerness to learn. "I'd love that. Thank you."

"Grab that stool over there and pull it up beside me. I'll explain the process."

His enthusiasm for sharing his work circled each word.

Amanda did as he instructed, but made sure not to sit too close. Even though the temperature had been set low in the lab, she still had to keep a safe distance from Lucius's fire.

He didn't speak loudly. His voice stayed low and smooth, almost reverent, as he explained in detail what he was doing and why.

"I'm working on two different trials. This one is dealing with women who have had cervical cancer and find their ability to reproduce severely compromised."

He went through all the particulars of the trial and his findings so far. "Do you have any questions?" he asked.

Amanda asked them and he patiently answered each one.

"Now, the other trial I'm working on is the use of Kisspeptin-LH compared to hCG. We're seeing great successes there."

Amanda didn't miss the pride in his voice. This man really cared about the work he did.

"My goal, in my lifetime, is to be able to increase our success rate in women having babies by fifty percent."

Amanda's eyes widened. "That is an ambitious goal."

He and his sister Kirri definitely came from the same family. When Kirri had first arrived in Atlanta she'd almost never come out of the lab. What had happened in their lives to make them so driven? It might have been a good thing—but everyone knew what happened if you had too much of a good thing…

Lucius turned earnest. "I know it's a lofty figure, but that's what it'll take for me to consider my work truly successful."

"I think even if you fall a little short you could still consider yourself successful."

"I'll only think I could have done better." His words sounded hard.

"Where did you get such drive?"

Lucius looked at her for a long moment, as if deciding if he wanted to answer or not. He turned to his test tubes once more.

"My father was a demanding man. He made it clear that he was disappointed if I didn't achieve. Failure was something he wouldn't accept."

Amanda nodded. She understood better now. "Kirri told me he was a doctor as well?"

"Yes—and he pretty much didn't leave us any choice except to be doctors as well."

He was still not facing her, and she had to lean in closer to hear him.

"Don't get me wrong—I love what I do. But my resistance to conformity by not following in his specialty has made it difficult at times. Worse, Kirri joined me and not him."

"I'm sure that having a father who required that much from you has helped make you the excellent doctor you are today," she said.

His gaze met hers. "Is that your way of seeing the cup half-full?"

She shrugged. "Better than half-empty. All you

have to do is look at those pictures in the lobby to know you were the one who was right."

That brought a smile to his face.

They spent another thirty minutes discussing the pros and cons of the work he had been doing in the trials. Then, too soon for her, Lucius put down the syringe, rolled the stool back and stood.

"I have a meeting in a few minutes, so that's it for today."

They walked out together and dropped their gowns in a barrel before entering the hallway.

"If I don't see you again, I'll pick you up at seven Saturday morning," Lucius said matter-of-factly.

"Do you still want to go?" Her voice shook. She cleared her throat.

"Don't you?" he asked.

"I just don't wanna put you out." Yeah, she *did* want to spend more time with this intriguing man.

"You're not putting me out. I swim there sometimes."

"Oh." So, he wasn't doing anything special by taking her. "I guess that's how you stay in such good shape."

"You think I'm in good shape?" His eyes twinkled.

Her cheeks warmed. Why couldn't she keep her mouth shout?

She walked away. "What I think is that I'll be ready at seven."

CHAPTER FOUR

LUCIUS HAD BEEN taught never to stand a woman up or back out on a date if at all possible. He'd failed miserably on both accounts where his wife had been concerned. More than once he'd taken it for granted that she would be there for him, or be at home regardless of whether or not he'd become caught up in his work. That had certainly contributed to his divorce.

Hoping he had learned from his mistakes, he arrived early to pick up Amanda on Saturday.

Of course the idea of canceling their swimming trip had crossed his mind. Yet his mother's lectures on manners whenever she came out of her book world had won out. So here he was, on this... Whatever it was, he didn't know. But he didn't want to call it a date.

He was well aware of feeling off-kilter, for the first time in a long while, but being around Amanda did that to him. When he'd considered their plans during the past week, he'd still wanted to take Amanda swimming. What he *didn't* want was to be feeling this powerful attraction to her.

Lucius wasn't a long-term relationship person. His failed marriage proved that. His needs, his job, had always come first. His career would always win out. His intense commitment to it made a traditional relationship impossible. In fact his devotion to his work meant his involvement with any woman would only be halfhearted at best. And from what he'd learned about Amanda she was an all-or-nothing person.

Lucius shook his head, trying to send such thoughts flying. Couldn't they be friends? Enjoy each other's company? Maybe share a kiss or two? No, that would never work. He wasn't even going to allow himself a chance to test that theory. It was a bad idea—of that he had no doubt.

What he would do was take Amanda swimming, and then keep his distance.

Feeling totally at a loss—which was a foreign emotion for him—he stood in front of Amanda's door. He prided himself on being master of his domain and in control of every situation. For some reason Amanda managed to make that impossible. He never knew what to expect from her. Their brief encounter at the picnic had more than put him off his normal "arm's length" strategy. Even his wife had never succeeded in derailing him from his established plans.

Amanda challenged him. She'd lured him out of his comfort zone when she had manipulated him into being the face in her pie-throwing contest. And somehow she'd gotten him to suggest she come swimming with him. The most startling realization of all was the fact that he actually enjoyed and even looked forward to their verbal sparring. He could let loose around Amanda like he never had with a woman before. He wasn't sure how she'd succeeded in putting him so much at ease, but she had.

Still, this had to stop—whatever "this" was.

When Amanda had joined him in the lab he had been impressed by how quick she had been to ask questions, along with how informed and thoughtful she was. Her interest hadn't seemed contrived. It had shown in her voice and in the intensity of her eyes. His work excited him and it was refreshing to find someone who shared that same passion. Amanda had seemed to hang on every word he spoke.

His wife hadn't ever done the same, despite having studied nursing. She'd shown no interest in his work. She hadn't wanted to listen to anything regarding what he had strived so hard to accomplish.

He'd finally realized, too late, that she'd gone into the field of medicine solely to find a doctor for a husband. She had been more interested in the social status and the money. As his fame in the world of infertility treatment had grown the more she'd liked it—until she hadn't.

He raised his fist to knock on Amanda's door. Before he could do so, it opened. He stepped back. Amanda stood there with her bag in her hand, wearing some type of flowing dress. Her hair had been pulled back, but several tendrils had come loose to frame her face.

"Hey…" she said uncertainly.

Surprised, he blurted, "How did you know I was here?"

"You're punctual. It's seven o'clock, so I figured you'd already be out here or you soon would be."

"Am I that predictable?" He wasn't sure he liked that idea.

She closed the door behind her. "Not in everything, but in being on time you are. I guess you're ready to go? I am." She started down the stairs. "Am I going to freeze to death, swimming in ocean water this early in the morning?"

Having no choice but to follow her, Lucius hurried down the steps. "You do know that temperatures here have been above thirty-two degrees Celsius and are supposed to go even higher today."

"Thirty-two? That's around ninety degrees Fahrenheit? But that doesn't mean the water is warm."

"I don't want you mad at me when you first get in, because it will be cool, but after you get moving you'll be just fine."

They stepped outside.

"I don't think it'll matter," she said. "I'm really looking forward to it. A pool like that is a novelty to me."

She swung the bag in her hand.

He directed her toward his car.

She came to a halt and studied his midnight-blue two-seater roadster. "I should've known this would be the type of car you'd drive."

Somehow that didn't sound like a compliment. "Is there something wrong with my car?"

It took Amanda a moment to answer as a grin crawled across her face. "Not a single thing. It is *too* sweet. To say that I like it would be an understatement."

Lucius swelled with pride. He opened the passenger door. "Get in and I'll take you for a ride."

"I wanna warn you I may hit you over the head and drive off with it if I get the chance."

Lucius chuckled, somehow feeling lighter. "Of course that would mean you'd be committing a felony."

"I've thought of that." She climbed in and ran a hand along the top of the door. "It would be totally worth it, though."

He closed her door and went around to slide into the driver's seat. "Should I call the police now?"

"I'll try to control myself at least until after I swim. I really want to see this pool."

Lucius started the car and drove away from the curb.

"How often do you go to this pool?" asked

Amanda. She had her head back, her eyes closed as the wind blew in her face.

"Whenever I want a change and can take the time to drive there. Otherwise I just swim at home."

"You have a pool at your house?" She rolled her head, looking at him.

"Yeah, but it isn't like the ones fed by the ocean." He shrugged. "And you agreed to come with me." For some reason that mattered to him. Too much.

Stop. Stop now. Remember the plan. Swim and take her home. No further involvement.

He turned his attention from Amanda to his driving as they passed through the neighborhood and out to the main road. Minutes later he moved onto the coastal road. Soon he pulled into the parking lot beside the competition-size pool. There were only a few other cars there that early in the morning.

Amanda stepped out, gathered her things, and met him at the rear of the car. Together they walked to the gate and went inside. They found a spot on the cement deck and put their belongings down.

Lucius slipped off his shoes and pulled his shirt over his head, leaving him in his swimming trunks. He looked at Amanda and she stared at him. It was like facing danger. His skin heated and his manhood shifted. Coming here with her was a bad idea.

He sharpened his resolve. "Are you going to swim or just watch me?" He needed to get in the cool water before his visceral reaction to her attention became visible. "If you decide to join me, I suggest you remove that dress."

He started for the pool, but not before he saw her come back to reality. He executed a shallow dive into the water. Thankfully, it *was* cool. He needed some help.

When he surfaced, he looked for Amanda. She'd removed her dress, leaving him with a full view of her in a black one-piece that was far sexier than any bikini would have been. The suit showed the cleavage between her full breasts, but only enough to tease him with the thought of what might be hidden. He followed the generous curves to hips that flared, leaving him in no doubt that she was all woman. Her legs were long and shapely, and made more so by the high cut of the suit's leg openings.

This swimming trip had been a bad idea in more ways than one. Amanda played havoc with his libido.

Shaking his head, trying to remove the befuddlement, he called, "Are you coming in?"

"On my way."

Amanda walked toward the steps and Lucius appreciated the subtle muscle movements of her body. *Graceful* would be the way he would describe it. *Sexy.*

He swallowed, bringing his focus back to where it should be. "Keep in mind this is salt water," he said.

Amanda eased down the steps until the water lapped at her waist, then plunged in. She proceeded to do a crawl stroke down the length of the pool.

Lucius joined her, keeping plenty of distance between them. They made another lap back, and then did it again. Amanda was a good swimmer, and she had excellent form.

She finally stopped at the corner of the pool and trod water. He joined her.

"This is absolutely amazing—wonderful." Amanda looked up at the sky. "It's like being in the ocean but *not* being in the ocean."

"I thought you'd like it."

He enjoyed watching her. She seemed to take so much pleasure in life. When was the last time he had stopped long enough to say that about himself?

"This is well hidden from tourists." She looked around. "I'm glad I had a chance to experience it."

"You're a good swimmer."

"Thank you." She continued to study the surrounding area as she said, "I was on the swim team in high school."

"It shows." Her movements through the water had been smooth and flowing.

"What did *you* do in high school?" she asked.

"I went to a boarding school. I was on the debate team."

"That figures."

He twisted his mouth. "Mostly I studied. My job was to make good grades so I could get into medical school."

She splashed at a spot on the wall. "I'd have to say my mom was a little more encouraging than that. I would've done more sport, but my stepfather didn't like paying for extracurricular activities. Specifically where I was concerned."

"Was money a problem?"

He knew she might consider the question rude, but he wanted to know more about her. He'd already told her more about himself than most people knew, and he'd only known her a couple of weeks.

"It had nothing to do with money. He just didn't want to spend it on *me*."

"Why was that?"

The desire to punch something filled him—preferably her stepfather, for treating her that way. His father might have been demanding, and rigid on all occasions, but Lucius and his sister had always known they were wanted.

"You know...the old story. Mother and daughter are a package deal, but he doesn't want the daughter because she reminds him that his wife loved someone else before him."

Amanda was trying to make light of it, but what he'd clearly heard in her voice was hurt.

"It was what it was," she said.

But that didn't make it right.

"Tell me about your father?"

"He died when I was very small. I don't remember him. All I know about him is what my mother has told me and a few pictures I've seen. My stepfather didn't like for my mother to talk about him. Still doesn't."

"How old were you when your mother remarried?"

Why was he asking all these questions? He didn't make a habit of delving into peoples' lives any more than he let them explore his. This wasn't putting the distance between them he'd promised himself he would start creating. Instead he was doing the reverse. He'd better get his act together soon.

"She remarried when I was two, then had my half-brother and sister. My stepfather didn't see me as a part of his responsibility or part of the family. One night I overheard him arguing with my mother about spending *his* money on a prom dress for me. In one way or another he always made it clear he considered me an outsider because I didn't carry his last name."

"Did your mother never consider changing your name to his?"

He groaned in his head. There—he'd done it again. But the draw to know more about her was great.

"I don't think so. She loved my father and wouldn't have dishonored him by doing that. And as I got older I wouldn't have let her. I always refused to be pushed around by my stepfather."

He bit his tongue, but the question got away from him anyway. "Did your half-brother and sister treat you differently?"

"No. We're very close. And they do notice how their father treats me. More than once they've taken up the issue with him for me."

"I'm glad to hear that."

He was. Her childhood must have been hard, yet she seemed to face the world with wonder and excitement.

"Enough serious talk," she said. "We have this wonderful pool to enjoy."

She began swimming again with a little more ferocity than before. Maybe she wasn't as unaffected by her past as she acted. It was as if she were trying to physically shove away those ugly years of being an outsider.

Lucius pushed off the wall and followed her across the pool. They made a few more laps and then Amanda stopped once more beside the wall closest to the ocean. He pulled up and joined her, placing a hand on the side of the pool while she trod water. The sun sparkled on the surface of the water and the ocean splashed against the rocks only feet away, producing a light spray.

Amanda raised her face. It was full of wonderment.

"You know, this really is an amazing place. I *love* Sydney."

Her words were breathy, as if she had swum too hard, and yet there was a kind of reverence to them.

"I'm going to pay close attention to how we get back to my apartment from here so I can come again by myself."

"How about I let you know when I'm coming and bring you along?"

"You would do that?"

That pleasure in her face became more pronounced.

"Sure—why not."

What had made him suggest *that*? He prided himself on his self-control and around Amanda he acted as if he had none. What was happening to him?

Amanda looked as if she was going to say something, but shook her head instead.

Suddenly a wave crashed against the rocks just outside the pool, splashing them. Amanda squealed, wiping water from her face. Seconds later she yelped again and pounced on him, wrapping her arms around his neck, moving her feet as if she wanted to climb him. He had to grip the wall with some force in order not to go under.

Finally Amanda calmed down enough to point as she hung on him. "What's *that*?"

Lucius chuckled. "That's just a baby squid who wanted to join us. He must have been washed over a minute ago."

Amanda's grip eased some, but she didn't let go and her focus remained on the happily swimming sea creature still not far away.

Settling her against him, he felt his mind and body become aware of the luscious woman in his arms. His gaze met hers. She blinked. To his satisfaction her total attention was now fixated on him. His gaze lowered to her slightly parted lips. Dewy drops puddled on her lower one. They looked as pink as the sunrise had been and plush as a pillow.

As bad an idea as he knew it was, he was driven to taste them. To experience them.

His mouth lowered to hers. She immediately joined him in the passion bubbling between them.

Amanda slid down and across him, so they were chest to chest. Her arms remained around his neck. He tightened his arm at her waist. Teasing her mouth with his tongue, he asked for entry and she freely gave it. So sweet, inviting, so enticing and addictive.

Her tongue joined his in a sensual dance.

His manhood lay thick between them.

The sound of someone giggling close by brought him back to where they were. He wasn't exactly a celebrity, but his face was frequently in the papers and on TV.

Reluctantly he broke off the kiss.

Amanda wore a dazed look. "Mmm…"

Her sound of disappointment sent a shot of satisfaction through him. Wow, the woman could kiss. He'd become rocket-hot with nowhere to go.

"We need to take this elsewhere. Families are starting to come in."

He turned her so she fit between him and the wall, protecting her from curious eyes. Seconds later he watched as her eyes cleared.

She peeked over his shoulder. "I…uh…guess we'd better."

He resisted taking her mouth again. Instead he reached out and cupped the squid, flinging it back over the wall into the ocean. "Thanks, little guy, you made a great wingman."

Amanda giggled and swam away.

He followed more slowly. If being around Amanda had already had him tied in knots, kissing her had sent his mind off into space. He had messed up—big-time. He needed to reaffirm his stance on having nothing to do with her. And after that kiss it would be far more difficult.

As she climbed out of the pool, Lucius took the opportunity to enjoy the view. When she reached their belongings, he called, "Would you mind bringing me my towel?"

She gave him a perplexed look, and then the reason must have dawned on her, because she gave him a mischievous grin. Picking up his towel, she brought it to the side of the pool. "Why, Doctor, do you need me to dry you off?"

Was there anything she wouldn't do or say? He gave a moment's thought to calling her bluff, but knowing Amanda she would do it just to prove a point.

"Thanks for the offer, but maybe later. Just drop it by the steps."

She made a show of letting it slip slowly through her fingers to puddle on the cement.

There wasn't any easy way to cover his arousal, so he made quick work of climbing out of the pool and wrapping the towel around his waist. By the time he turned to Amanda she'd pulled on her flowing dress and had her bag in hand.

"You going to be able to drive, Doc?" A grin still curved her mouth.

"I am—but if you want to, you can." He started toward the car with her beside him.

Amanda's eyebrows went toward her hairline and her eyes widened. "Really?"

"If you'd like to. But I'm not sure a woman who's afraid of a baby squid can handle it."

Turnabout was fair play. He could tease as well.

But something was certainly off with him. He

didn't normally tease *anyone*. Kirri would never believe it.

"I can assure you that I can handle it. The squid just surprised me."

He nodded thoughtfully. "Enough that you climbed up me like I was a tree?"

"I did not!"

Lucius chuckled. "Now, you see, it depends on who's the climb*ee* and who's the climb*er*."

"Are you making fun of me?" Amanda glared at him.

"No, I'd never do that." He dangled his car keys between them.

Something really was wrong with him. But he liked it. A lot. Their banter made him feel lighter, somehow.

She grinned and snatched the keys from his hand. A few minutes later they were belted in and Amanda had revved the motor. With a grin at him, she put the car into gear and drove out of the parking lot.

Lucius watched the pure joy on her face as they moved along the windy coast road on their return to the city. He'd never before let anyone else drive his car. His mouth pursed for a moment. Whatever was happening between them, it had to stop here, before it got out of hand.

"For this, I'll fix you breakfast," she announced as she made a turn.

He wasn't sure he should agree to that. But he wouldn't hurt her feelings by telling her no. Maybe he could get out of it diplomatically.

"You cook?"

"Of course I do. I'm a good cook. As good as I am a driver."

She smiled at him.

A smile that reached into his gut and tugged.

He'd been the one to put that happy expression on her face. The feeling was nice, adding a bit of zeal to his life and, in an odd way, contentment. He enjoyed Amanda's company—even the teasing. With her, some of the weariness of his life seemed to slip away. Come to think of it, he hadn't thought about the clinic, or his work in hours. Surely breakfast together wouldn't hurt anyone?

"You're going to have to give me directions. Good ones. Because I'm driving on a different side of the road and I have to think about that."

"You want me to take over?"

Her chin jutted out and her determined eyes met his for a second. "Not a chance."

"You want to turn left in about a mile."

With a smile on his face he couldn't explain he continued to watch her and give directions for the next fifteen minutes.

Just another hour with Amanda wouldn't matter. How could it?

* * *

Amanda loved Lucius's car. Only in her dreams would she ever have thought she'd even get to ride in so fine a car, but to drive it was beyond her imagination.

More than that, she couldn't believe with how much abandon she'd reacted to Lucius's kiss. Worse was the fact she'd jumped into his arms like a silly schoolgirl.

She had been bold. Too bold.

That was an understatement.

She'd even gone so far as to invite him to breakfast.

But Lucius wasn't just some fellow visiting the clinic, or one of the local men who wanted a night out. He was intense, dedicated, serious, driven… The list went on. And she'd been teasing him. Had gone so far as to make fun of his discomfort at the pool when he'd become aroused. Had she lost her mind?

Lucius wasn't the type of man she should be attracted to. She'd never let anyone close enough to get truly serious—couldn't trust men. They had let her down too many times in her life. Her father had died, her stepfather had never been there for her, and the last guy she'd cared about had ended up being a jerk. She couldn't survive another man disappointing her at this point in her life.

But surely she and Lucius were just friends.

Why couldn't they enjoy a swim and breakfast together without it getting complicated?

Maybe because of that kiss...

Perhaps she shouldn't have invited him to eat, but it was too late now.

She drove up the street where she lived. Stunned, she saw several work trucks lined it, right in front of her apartment building. There were people standing around in groups, watching whatever was happening.

"Pull up over there." Lucius pointed to a spot behind one of the trucks. "Then we'll see what's going on."

She did as he said, then handed the keys to Lucius and grabbed her bag, not waiting for him. The first person she came to, she asked, "What's wrong?"

"Fire sprinkler went off."

"Was there a fire?" Lucius asked from beside her.

"No. Just a sprinkler malfunction," the man said. "But it's made a real mess. The building will have to be condemned."

"Condemned? Where am I going to live?" She wasn't speaking to anyone in particular as she walked closer to the apartment building. "I don't know of anyplace this close to the clinic. Not even a hotel."

Lucius had remained beside her. "You can stay at my house until we figure something out."

She stopped and gave him a look of disbelief. "What? I can't *live* with you."

He said in a flat voice, "I said *stay*. I have the space. It'll at least give you a place for the weekend. A place to regroup. Figure things out."

"I don't know... Let me see if all of this is true."

She kept moving toward her building, dodging all the people. When she reached the front door she saw the man she knew as the apartment supervisor standing there.

"Mr. Kent—what's going on?"

The man looked haggard, and he confirmed what she had been told. "They're going to give us a half an hour to get what we can out of our apartments, then close the entire building up."

Just then a firefighter stepped out of the building and said, "Those who live here can go in for thirty minutes and get what they can. No longer. Please be prepared to show your identification."

Amanda stepped forward. The supervisor vouched for her and she vouched for Lucius when he stated he would be going up with her.

Minutes later, glad she had on shoes that were appropriate for water, she splashed through the front hall and up the stairs. Opening her apartment door, she looked dumbfounded at the soggy mess the apartment had become. She could only imagine what it would smell like when the heat of the day arrived...

"What can I do to help?" Lucius asked from behind her.

She picked up her new pillows, despite them being wet, and pulled them to her chest.

"Amanda, you don't have much time."

Compassion filled his voice, but there was a firmness as well. That was enough to get her moving.

"Tell me what to do." Lucius sounded sterner now.

"There are some plastic bags under the cabinet. Get some and put these pillows and that vase in them. I'll get my clothes."

She went to the bedroom, not waiting on Lucius to respond. She did have an advantage over the other residents in that she didn't live there permanently. Most of what she owned would fit into her suitcase, except what she'd told Lucius to pick up. To her surprise he hadn't argued or said that they were trivial items and should be left behind.

He stood in the doorway. "Is there anything else you want to get?"

"Get those two boxes of macaroni and cheese from the cabinet next to the microwave."

"You can replace those. That's not important." His voice held exasperation.

"I know, but I want them."

She didn't look at him but continued throwing her clothes into her suitcase, willy-nilly. Moments later she closed it. Lucius had returned and he took the case from her, handing her the plastic bags he carried.

"Ready?"

She nodded sadly. The apartment had only been her home for a couple of weeks, but it had been *hers*.

They stomped downstairs, being careful not to slip. Lucius led her back to the car and put her belongings in the trunk. He opened the passenger door and held it until she sat. Then he drove her away in a direction she didn't know.

With it being the weekend, she had no choice but to go with him or go to a hotel. How else would she get to the clinic if she was needed? But why had she let Lucius convince her to go with him so easily?

Because she was weak where he was concerned. And she trusted him. It was something she didn't easily do, yet Lucius had managed to earn her trust quickly.

"You can stay at my place until we figure something else out. I have three spare bedrooms. One is really a suite. You can stay there."

Less than an hour ago she'd been kissing him like there would be no tomorrow. There had been nothing friendly about it. Not that she hadn't enjoyed every second of it. And now she was going to stay at his house.

The idea spelled disaster. At least for her. What if he tried to kiss her again?

Surely she could handle herself like an adult for the weekend? She wasn't a teenage girl who'd been asked by the most popular boy in school to go to the prom. She needed a place to stay. It had been a practical decision. Lucius was just being friendly and supportive. Since she technically worked for him, he probably felt responsible for her.

She wouldn't make more of this invitation than there was. What she needed to do was focus on why she was here in Sydney.

They sat in silence as Lucius drove around the harbor.

"I didn't realize you lived so far from the clinic." She looked out at the sailboats filling the water on this weekend morning.

"Since I was a boy I've been fascinated by my house. When it came on the market I bought it. It's worth the drive."

She enjoyed the view of all the homes by the water. Then they entered another affluent neighborhood, left it, and drove on into one that looked slightly less expensive.

Finally Lucius pulled onto a white graveled driveway. A manicured privacy hedge stood on each side. The drive circled through a well-tended yard of green grass. A sprawling white nineteen-sixties one-story brick house came into view.

Lucius stopped the car in front of double wooden doors. Two large urns holding tall green plants were stationed on either side. Everything was in its place.

"This looks just like a place where you'd live," she said. She loved it immediately. Something about it said *home*.

"I'm not sure that's a compliment… It sounds suspiciously like what you said about my car. I'm clearly a man who holds no surprises."

That certainly wasn't true. Their kiss had proved it.

She licked her lips. "Yeah, but you know I like your car."

"You have made that clear."

His eyes lingered on her mouth. Finally he broke the moment and climbed out. Going to the trunk, he unloaded her things.

"Did your clothes get wet?" he asked.

"They're more like damp."

"We'll get them in the wash right now."

He unlocked the front door and pushed it wide. "Welcome to my home."

Amanda forced herself not to gasp. The wide and spacious entrance with its high ceiling and gleaming oak floors took her breath away. Ahead was a glass wall that looked out onto a green lawn, and the view of the harbor beyond overtook her amazement at the foyer. She could tell why he liked this house so much. It was a piece of heaven.

Lucius led her down a short hallway that opened

into a sunken living room. In it were a couple of brown leather sofa units and a large TV hung on a white brick wall. The understated luxury looked comfortable and very masculine. From here she could clearly see the Opera House and the Sydney Bridge.

"Wow!" The sound rushed from her.

"The laundry is this way."

Lucius moved along another hallway running parallel with the back wall. They were soon in a kitchen that had the same breathtaking view. A small room that branched off it held the washer and the dryer.

"I want to do the pillows first, so they can get as much drying time outside as possible."

Lucius lifted the lid of the washer. "Why're these so important to you?"

"Because I bought them to make the space mine." She shrugged. "I don't know... I just like them." She blinked, trying to keep the moisture filling her eyes at bay. Why was she so upset over an apartment that really wasn't hers?

Lucius must have noticed, because he pulled her into his arms for a hug. She let him. Just for a moment surely it would be okay.

"I know you must be rattled by all this. First a squid and now your apartment..."

She pulled back. "Don't you dare make fun of me!"

"I'm not. I promise." He pulled her back to his

chest, then let her go. "I tell you what—why don't I find you something dry to wear so you can get out of that bathing suit? Then I'll show you your bedroom and I'll cook you breakfast—or lunch. Whichever you prefer. Then you can just hang around here and watch TV, swim or sleep. I'm sure things will look better in an hour or two."

She didn't want to agree but it all sounded wonderful. A hot bath, dry clothes and time for a think would be great. Having someone take care of her for a change had its appeal. She didn't usually allow that. Most of the men she'd dated complained she could be too independent.

"Okay, point me in the right direction."

Lucius led her back across the house to the other side of the living room. He opened a door, revealing a spacious room with another view of the harbor. A large bed with a striped bedspread took center-stage. A sitting area lay off to one side, and it included a small TV.

He'd seemed to imply earlier that the suite would be more like a maid's quarters. It turned out to be much nicer and spacious than that. She could get used to staying here—but she wouldn't.

"The bathroom is through that door. Take your time. I'll leave you some clothes on the bed."

Amanda sighed. She'd have a tough time leaving this place to go live in a hotel—or anywhere else for that matter.

"I hope you'll be comfortable here."

"Are you kidding? This is amazing. I don't know how you go to work every day when you could stay here and just *be*."

Could she do that? Just *be* for the next couple of days? Could she live harmoniously with him and the sexual tension that sizzled between them whenever they were near each other? Would it grow to become more than she could resist? Especially since all she had to do was look at Lucius to think of their kiss in the pool and his noticeable reaction to it. She'd seen the thickness of his manhood before he'd covered himself.

"I admit the view did have a lot to do with me buying the house. But it's only really nice if you have somebody to share it with."

"I'll be glad to share it with you. Anytime. Like I said, it's amazing."

That had sounded more suggestive that it should have...

"Then today we'll enjoy it together," he said.

And with that promise he left her.

There was a real chance she'd agreed to enter the lion's den. If she didn't keep her wits about her she would get bitten.

CHAPTER FIVE

LUCIUS WONDERED IF his feelings resembled those of a soldier who had invited the enemy into his camp. Not that he considered Amanda his *enemy*, as such. It was more he was unsure of what to expect. The problem was his attraction to her. He'd tried not to be, yet he had failed miserably.

Still, she was homeless. He had the room, so it had seemed logical and gentlemanly to ask her if she wanted to stay with him for the time being. Unsure about the situation, but in a strange country, Amanda hadn't put up much resistance to his suggestion.

While she remained under his roof he must keep his hands to himself, despite his desire to grab her, kiss her and haul her off to his bed. He couldn't remember being this infatuated with a woman—ever. Their kiss had assured him that there was something special between them.

Not even his wife had held the type of lure for him that Amanda did. Maybe that was because he knew she'd soon be leaving. That there would be no long-term commitment. He'd failed miserably at his marriage and had no intention of doing that again. Nothing about him had changed to make him think he'd be any different from how he had been the first time around. He wouldn't put any woman through that kind of agony.

He'd accepted what his job would require, what his world would look like, when he'd become a doctor. He had been raised to believe that was how he should live, knowing his priorities. Success had brought even more demands on him, but he did good in the world and that was important. Last Saturday's picnic had proved that.

Because of his responsibilities he couldn't promise Amanda anything, but did that mean they couldn't enjoy each other's company before she left, though? They liked each other, had their work in common, and were both fond of swimming. There was also their witty conversation and the fun they had together.

Fun? No one had ever accused him of being a *fun* person. He was rather surprised he was even capable of it. But Amanda made him happy. When was the last time he'd been able to say that?

Would she agree to a fling or just want to remain friends? He couldn't ever offer more than that.

Lucius had almost finished preparing breakfast when Amanda came into the kitchen. He had to reinforce his resolution when she came near, freshly showered and with pink cheeks. She wore one of his T-shirts and a pair of his shorts that were far too big for her. He guessed she wore nothing beneath them, which did absolutely nothing to tamp down his desire.

Amanda sniffed the air. "That smells wonderful."

She did too.

"Hey, how're you feeling?" he asked.

"Better. Just hungry."

He moved the pan off the hot stove. "That's good. It's ready. I went with making breakfast, since I'm a little better at cooking that than I am the other meals of the day."

She giggled.

The sound did something to Lucius in an area of his chest he didn't recognize.

"I could've fixed it."

He inhaled her scent, storing it in his memory. "I've got it. I'll give you a chance to prove you're a good cook another time."

"I could do supper tonight." She sounded eager.

"I thought we'd order in Chinese and watch a movie. It'd be a lot less work."

Amanda stepped around him. "But I—"

"No argument. You rest today and then we'll see about tomorrow."

"You *do* know you can't tell me what to do outside of work?"

There was strength in her words, but a note of playfulness as well. Although one thing he had learned early on was that Amanda didn't like taking orders outside the clinic.

"I do know that. Now, if you wish, *please* pick up your plate and take it outside to the table by the pool and breakfast will be served."

"That's more like it."

Amanda, with a huge smile on her face, took the plate he had just filled with food. She led the way out the door. He followed with his own plate.

"This is very decadent." Amanda placed the plate on the table.

"I've never thought of it like that." He hadn't. This was simply the way he lived his life.

"That's because you're used to having a pool in the side yard and a beautiful view of the harbor. Living in Atlanta, among a lot of high-rise buildings and with the coast hours away, I never eat in a place like this."

"Still, I wouldn't describe it as decadent…"

"Look at this." She waved her hand around. "Even the plants are perfect."

"If it'll make you feel more comfortable I'll throw a few napkins in among them."

Laughter burst from Amanda. Lucius joined in. It felt so good to laugh. He'd not known enough of that in his life. He intended to enjoy it while he could.

Amanda settled down to giggles and worked words in around them. "I'm sorry. I'm being a poor guest. It's just that I'm so impressed. You have a lovely home."

"Thank you. Now, what would you like to

drink? I only have coffee, tea, and water until I call in my grocery list."

"You have your groceries delivered, don't you?"

"Yes. Is that a problem?"

She pressed her lips together, as if she was making an effort not to grin. "Nope. Hot tea sounds perfect."

"I'll be right back. Go ahead and eat so it won't get cold."

It had been a long time since he'd been a host. He rarely had company, and when he did it was usually a business gathering and he hired a catering service to handle the food. He found it refreshing to show hospitality personally.

This morning he was doing all types of things out of the ordinary for him.

Returning to Amanda, he found her sitting in her chair with her head back and her eyes closed. She straightened as he approached. He placed their drinks on the table.

"I'm sorry. Again, I'm not being much of a guest if I go to sleep on you."

"No problem. You've had an unusual few hours and swimming can tire you as well. After you eat your breakfast feel free to take a nap."

"I have to admit that cushioned lounger looks inviting…" She looked past him toward the pool.

He picked up his fork. "It's all yours. I have paperwork that I need to attend to."

She started on her food when he did. "Do you work all the time?"

He hadn't thought about it, but now that he did he realized he *did* work much of the time. That was what he knew—it had been the example his father had set for him.

"A good deal of it, yes."

"You *do* know that it's okay to take time off as well? It'll make you a better doctor."

Lucius studied her for a moment. "Is that your prescription for a problem I don't know that I have? I'm used to using my time constructively."

His family measured success by how busy they were. They believed in producing results.

"I'm sorry. The way you live your life isn't my business." She returned to her meal.

They continued to eat in silence.

Amanda cleared her plate and placed her fork down.

"Why don't you go on and get that nap?" Lucius said.

"I can't leave you with the dishes—you cooked."

"Don't worry about them."

"Then that lounger is calling me. Breakfast was great, thank you."

"My pleasure. Just be sure that you don't get too much sun." He started gathering the dishes.

"I understand about the Australian sun. I'll get my sunscreen and a hat."

Sometime later he looked out the kitchen window to see Amanda settled on the lounger. She looked relaxed. What would it hurt if he joined her for a while? Work could wait...

He frowned. If he wasn't careful she would corrupt him.

Amanda woke to the sound of soft snores beside her. She looked to her right to see Lucius lying on the lounger next to her. He wore no shirt and dark sunglasses covered his eyes. She studied him. He was a handsome man, with his tanned body, square jaw, and wavy hair that begged to be touched. The temptation to run her hand through it almost overcame her.

He was a combination of toughness and sensitivity. She'd seen for herself this large man holding a tiny baby with such tenderness. He tried so hard not to show that side of himself, yet she'd seen it again today when she'd lost her apartment. He'd been really sweet and understanding, treating her like a queen.

She'd better get her defense shields up if she was going to keep some space between them. The enigma he was had a powerful pull on her. One she feared would hurt her when it was time for her to leave. She couldn't stand another heartache.

Amanda shifted on the cushions. The slight difference in his breathing told her Lucius had woken, yet he remained still.

"Amanda, are you watching me?" His voice

had turned gravelly from sleep and sounded super-sexy.

She shivered. What would it be like to hear it in her ear as he entered her?

She cleared her throat. *Whoa,* her imagination was working overtime.

"Uh…yes. I've been thinking that maybe we should have some ground rules while I'm staying here."

"Ground rules?" His tone was now cautious and suspicious. "Like no staring at me while I sleep?"

Heat that had nothing to do with the Australian sun filled her cheeks. She licked her lips. "That one could be added."

"I don't care if you look at me. I find it flattering."

He still hadn't turned in her direction, but she could see a hint of a smile on his mouth.

She needed to bring this conversation back to where it belonged. "I was thinking more like if I'm going to stay here, even for a little while, we need to have an understanding. After that kiss…"

"You didn't like it?" His voice held a teasing note.

Heat rushed through her. "I didn't say that."

Lucius rolled toward her. "Then you *did* like it?"

"I just don't think it should happen again." She had quickly lost control of this discussion.

"Why not?" He still watched her.

"Uh… I just think that sort of stuff will confuse things." This wasn't going well at all. "I don't want us to get uncomfortable with each other. I think we need to keep this friendly and uncomplicated. What happened at the pool doesn't need to be repeated."

She couldn't see his blue eyes for the dark sunglasses, but she could easily imagine them snapping.

"Let's forget the ground rules all except one," he said.

"Lucius, hear me out—"

"Look, I'm attracted to you, but I'm not going to do anything you don't agree with. It's as simple as that. If you want more than just us being 'friendly,' as you put it, you only have to say the word. It's all up to you. If you don't, I'll learn to live with it. Now, does that ease your mind?"

Amanda swallowed. For some reason Lucius's attitude left her bereft. It was as if the idea of remaining friends with her or not didn't matter to him one way or another. Here she was, struggling to keep her distance for both their sakes, and he was acting flippant about it.

"Okay…" Even to her own ears it sounded weak.

Lucius nodded and settled back on the lounger. Silence hung between them. It didn't feel friendly. If anything, their discussion had escalated the tension between them. She glanced at Lucius. His arms rested over his waist and his ankles were crossed as if all was well with his world. Meanwhile hers whirled with turmoil.

She looked out over the harbor at the boats and the ferries moving across the water. Somehow it eased her nerves. Being in Australia, even with Lucius, was good for her. Life back home had been all about work and proving herself for too long. Here she sat, in this time and place, just enjoying the warmth of the sun.

Sometime later Lucius stood. "Okay, enough sun. Time to go in."

Amanda started to argue but knew he was right. She didn't need to burn. She followed him inside.

"Make yourself at home in the kitchen. I've got work to do. I'll see you later." Lucius left her without a backward glance.

Amanda went to her room and caught up on some reading, then quietly prepared herself a sandwich for lunch. She thought about doing one for Lucius too, but she didn't know him well enough to know what he preferred, or even if he ate anything at lunchtime, so she decided to let it go.

The sun had started to go down when he came to her open door and stopped. "Hey, I was just getting ready to call for some Chinese. You still good with that?"

"That'll be great."

Amanda wanted to groan. Her response had sounded far too eager. But she'd not seen him since the morning and in an odd way she'd missed him. The air seemed less electrified with him not around. Lucius gave her chills, but in a good way.

Ooh, she needed to stop those kinds of thoughts. She was in Sydney to *work*, not to start a relationship with a man, and certainly not with one with such a high profile.

"You won't require the movie to be a chick flick, will you?"

She put an indignant note in her voice. "I like other movies as well."

"Good to know. I'll go call for the Chinese. I'll let you know when it's here." He turned and left.

The evening soon developed into a nice one. They agreed on a *Bourne* movie, and she took one couch and he the other. Lucius had surround sound, so watching the movie resembled being at a real theater. It turned out he even had automatic drapes installed over the huge windows. When they were closed darkness surrounded them, like being in a cave.

Amanda tried to get caught up in the movie but she couldn't seem to get beyond the knowledge that the sexy man who had kissed her like there was no tomorrow sat only feet away.

Her attention kept drifting Lucius's way. A couple of times he caught her looking at him and raised a brow, before his attention returned to the movie. In a way, it made her mad. Here she was, with her nerves in knots and firing overtime, and Lucius sat there as cool as could be. It was wrong. It made her want to rattle his cage.

Before she went to bed, she opened the door to the patio off her room and stepped outside. The lights of Sydney reflected off the harbor. The Opera House looked like full white sails and the bridge twinkled in the velvet of the night. The sound of splashing drew her attention to the pool. Apparently Lucius was swimming. Hadn't he gotten enough exercise that morning or was he swimming for another reason?

Maybe he hadn't been as unaffected by her presence as he had acted. She discovered she really liked that idea.

Lucius woke with a jolt to sounds coming from the kitchen. Someone was in there.

Amanda.

He should've realized that right away, since he'd spent most of the night trying to forget she was sleeping just on the other side of the house.

He'd swum and swum, hoping exhaustion would take him after spending the evening watching a movie with her just a few steps away. Done with his swim, he'd taken a shower—a cold one—and still his body hadn't settled down. He'd tossed and turned into the wee hours of the morning before he'd finally found some rest.

He'd taken a big risk by inviting her into his home. The problem was he hadn't thought it through well enough. Hell, he hadn't thought *at all*. He'd just opened his mouth and the words had come out. There had been no consideration about what it would do to his mind or his body to have her so close twenty-four-seven.

He was a man who had accepted his solitude long ago, but it hadn't taken Amanda long to disrupt it. She made him want things that had long lain dormant and should remain that way. The sooner she was out of his house the better.

Normally he rose early, but thoughts of Amanda had managed to get his life out of sync. Even something as simple as a night's sleep had become problematic. But her pull on him had to ease sometime, surely? Maybe he would be able to get beyond this—whatever "this" was—if he kissed her again. Just once more.

But he had made a promise. One that he would honor even though it might be the death of him.

He climbed out of bed and pulled on shorts and a T-shirt, then headed for the kitchen. Amanda stood at the counter with her back to him. His first instinct was to slip up behind her and kiss her neck. But as enticing as the thought might be, he held himself in check. He might regret being a gentleman but...

Amanda looked over her shoulder as she continued to butter bread. "Mornin'."

He loved her accent, and the sound of her voice when she dropped the last letter of a word. Somehow hearing it made having to get out of bed something to look forward to.

"Good morning."

"I hope I didn't wake you? I'm making toast and eggs. Want some?"

"Yes, I do. I'm hungry."

His gaze met hers and held. Did she realize it was her he was hungry for?

"I'll have it ready in a few minutes."

It had been a long time since he'd woken to find a woman in his kitchen. He found he liked it. Having someone else in the house was nice. Or was it having *Amanda* there?

How had he let his thoughts, imagination and libido get so out of hand? Hadn't it been just yesterday morning when he had planned to put some distance between them?

Yeah, that had been before that kiss that had left him dreaming of more and before he'd brought her home with him. He was a gentleman, not a monk.

Amanda glanced at him. "Did you sleep well?"

He couldn't answer that honestly, so he gave up and lied. "I did."

"Good. I wanted to ask you about how close the ferry port is to here." She continued to work.

"I'll be glad to drive you anywhere you need to go."

She'd already started shaking her head. "No, I want to ride the ferry. See the city and the surrounding area from the water."

"I've not been on the ferry since I was a boy."

"Then you should come too."

Amanda smiled at him as if it was the perfect solution to a problem he hadn't been aware he had.

Lucius knew he should say no, but he couldn't think of a good reason not to go.

"Okay. While you finish breakfast I'll check the ferry schedule."

"Sounds like a plan." She picked up an egg and broke it over a bowl.

A couple of hours later they were on their way out the front door, Amanda almost bouncing with enthusiasm. Lucius followed with a lot less excitement. He knew he was quickly moving out of his comfort zone and creating more problems for himself.

"How far is it to the ferry port?" she wanted to know.

"I guess about a half a mile."

"It's a nice day—let's walk. The weather report said it wasn't going to rain until later tonight."

He twisted his mouth, lowered his chin and looked at her in amazement. "You listened to the weather report?"

"Yeah, I turned on the radio while I was dressing. Where I come from during the spring and summer we have rain almost every day, so you have to plan."

"I really don't mind driving." He hadn't walked any distance in years.

"I like to walk. It lets you see things you wouldn't when you're riding by. I want to really *see* the neighborhood."

"All right."

Lucius figured he wasn't going to win the argument. From the sound of it she had already made her mind up. He'd quickly learned that she had a tendency to do that.

Strolling down the driveway, they soon reached the sidewalk. They passed a few people. A couple jogged by while others walked their dogs. To his astonishment Amanda spoke to everyone. After their initial surprise they returned her greeting.

"Why do you do that?" he asked.

"What?" Amanda asked over her shoulder as she looked through the gateway of a house.

"Speak to everyone?"

She shrugged and joined him again. "Just being friendly, I guess. It's what we do at home. We make eye contact when we come up to someone and then we speak. I thought everyone did it."

He grinned. "You're shocking my neighbors."

Her eyes widened and she cocked her head to the side in surprise. "Really? Should I stop?"

"No, they'll recover. It sounds like a nice habit to have."

She grinned. "I guess it's a Southern thing."

"I thought maybe you were going to tell me it was an Amanda thing." He found there were a number of things he considered special about her.

"I wasn't gonna say that." She glanced over her shoulder at him.

"Gonna? I like the way you phrase things. Your accent and the slow way you speak. Somehow it's soothing."

"Thank you. But I don't want you to think because I talk slow I think slow."

They turned a corner.

"I would never make that mistake," he said. "You're one of the most intelligent people I know."

"Why, Dr. West, I do believe you're trying to charm me. Thank you. I consider that high praise coming from you," she said in a distracted voice as she studied the house they were passing. "The houses around here are amazing. Everyone takes such meticulous care of them and their lawns."

"Here I was thinking you were super-impressed just with my house."

She grabbed his forearm. "Oh, I am. I really am. It's close to perfect."

"I might have fished for that compliment, but I'll take it."

He liked hearing that Amanda admired his home. He wanted her to like it. And that really was somewhere he didn't need to go. He would never offer another woman a permanent place in his life *or* his home. No, he wouldn't do that to himself or to the woman. He would only end up disappointing her, and that was something he never wanted to do again.

They took another turn and he could see the ferry port up ahead. He rarely used public transportation of any kind. The ferry would be as much a novelty for him as for Amanda.

He paid for their tickets and they walked on.

Amanda led him upstairs. "I want a good spot."

He looked around. Few people were on board. It was Sunday morning and not as busy as it would be on a week-day, when people were traveling to work.

"I don't think that'll be a problem," he said.

"I think you're making fun of me again."

He grinned. "I'd never do that."

Amanda gave his arm a light swat. "I know you would."

The ferry moved out into the harbor. As it did so they stood in silence for a while, just looking around them.

"This is really amazing," Amanda said, as much to the wind as she did to him. "We have nothing like this close to where I live. I do have a friend who lives on a houseboat on one of the lakes nearby, though."

Lucius crossed his arms and leaned on the rail.

"I'm not sure that would be a great place to be during a storm."

"You're probably right. Do you ever take the ferry to work?"

"No, I can't take that kind of time. I can be there much faster driving."

"I think it would be a lovely way to start the day—riding across the water, then walking to work. Relaxing before the craziness of the day starts."

That had never occurred to Lucius. He rose every morning thinking about what he had to do that day. He didn't have time for a leisurely trip to work. Or at least he'd never thought he had.

"That might pose a problem, since babies aren't known for waiting around on ferries."

"That would be the case for me, but less for you. You schedule your procedures."

She had him there. "So, what're we going to do when we get to the other side?" he asked.

Amanda giggled.

"What's so funny?" It had sounded like a reasonable question to him.

"That just made me think of an old joke."

"What joke?"

"You know the one. Why did the chicken cross the road? To get to the other side!"

He chuckled. "I get it. We're riding the ferry to get to the other side."

"Yes, but I'd like to go to that mall, the Strand,

and see the stained-glass I've heard about. You're welcome to come with me."

He hadn't been there since he was a boy. His mother had taken him and his sister. His father had had little time for such outings. Even if he had the mall would have been the last place his father would have agreed to go. He was more of a museum kind of person.

Why *shouldn't* Lucius go with Amanda? The seminar notes he had to prepare for the medical conference next month could wait. He'd been doing things out of character since he'd met Amanda, so what would one more matter?

"If you don't mind me tagging along?"

"I'd like to have you join me."

She gave him a bright smile.

Suddenly his day seemed more cheerful.

The time went by surprisingly fast.

After they'd exited the ferry they strolled along the brick walk surrounding the harbor and then started toward the Strand. It was great fun to watch Amanda's face light up as she experienced the city for the first time.

At the mall, she looked up at the stained-glass ceiling in delight. "It's awesome."

Lucius couldn't help but smile. "You sure are using that word often."

"I guess I am. I think most of the things in Australia are amazing."

His chest area warmed when her eyes drifted

to him. He didn't know if she was truly including him, but he hoped she was. He liked to think Amanda was flirting with him.

"How about lunch while we're here?"

They found a small café with tables and chairs outside the front door. There they ate their sandwiches. Afterward they walked back toward the ferry port.

As they passed a small grocery store Amanda grabbed his arm. "I need to go in here for a few minutes. I want to get some things for that supper I promised you."

"Why don't you wait and I'll have them delivered?"

She shook her head. "It's just one or two things. And I like to pick out my own produce."

"Okay."

Lucius followed her in. He hadn't been in a grocery store in years.

Amanda grabbed a plastic basket and started down the narrow aisle. She picked out a bundle of asparagus, some eggs, and located a package of brownie mix.

"I'd get some ice cream but it wouldn't make it home."

He took the basket from her. "I already have some at home."

"That figures," she said.

He placed the basket on the bench to check out. "How's that?"

She grinned. "You're a man. Most men consider ice cream a staple."

"I'm not sure I like being lumped in with 'most' men, but I do like ice cream."

She insisted on paying. Then she said, "I'm ready to go home now."

Amanda calling his place "home" left another warm feeling in his chest.

He frowned. In a few weeks she would be going back to America. He must be desperate for female attention to be acting like a giddy schoolboy with his first crush.

Lucius took the bags from her as they left the store.

"I like being able to get my groceries and walk home," she said. "We do too much driving where I live."

They made it to the ferry just as it was docking. This time they rode on the inside. They talked some, but also sat in silence. As they were getting off he took the bags once more. Amanda put up a small argument but soon relented.

At the house, she insisted she'd put their purchases away. He went to his office to check for messages.

It had been an amazing day. Exploring the city with Amanda had been fun. Instead of being tired from the exercise he felt invigorated. He'd seen his home city through different eyes.

In future he would make time to have more days like this one.

It just wouldn't be with Amanda.

Amanda placed a pan of water on the stove. When had she last cooked dinner for a man? It had been a long time. She found it satisfying. It gave her a sense of being needed. That was something she had always wanted but rarely felt. On the selfish side, and deep down, she acknowledged that had been part of the reason she'd gone into nursing. There she was definitely needed.

But, regardless of how nice it felt, she shouldn't get used to preparing Lucius's meals. Doing so was temporary, a onetime thing, and nothing more. They'd had a lovely day together, but just as friends. That was the way it should be.

Right now she trusted no man not to hurt her. She wanted forever. So far no man had offered her that. Lucius hadn't given any indication he'd ever be that man, so why have all these unrealistic thoughts about him? His friendship would have to be enough.

He had offered to barbecue the steaks while she worked inside on the rest of the meal. She was happy to have his help. He came in as she finished mixing the brownies.

"The steaks will be done in a few minutes." He grabbed a platter.

"That'll be about the time I have everything

else ready. Do you think it's too hot for us to eat outside?"

"We'll be fine under the umbrella."

"Great. I'm jealous of where you get to spend your time. I'm trying to soak up all I can before I have to leave."

He smiled. "You're welcome to it."

A quarter of an hour later Amanda had everything together. She'd set the table and was now carrying out a plate of asparagus and a bowl of macaroni and cheese.

Lucius waited at the table with the steaks nearby. "Looks good." He took the bowl from her and placed it on the table. He gave it an unconvinced look.

She narrowed her eyes. "You're surprised?"

"Let's just say it's unexpected."

"I think that's a diplomatic way of dodging my question. May I fix you a plate?"

"Please." He handed her his plate and she placed a scoop of macaroni and cheese on it along with a bundle of asparagus.

She passed him her own empty plate. "Steak, please."

Lucius forked one piece of meat onto her plate and the other onto his. Amanda added portions of the rest of the food to hers, sat down, and pushed the basket of rolls toward Lucius. He took one.

She watched as Lucius initially moved his macaroni and cheese around, as if still unsure. Finally he placed a forkful in his mouth and chewed.

"Not bad. Better than I thought it would be." He sounded surprised.

She snorted in amusement.

"That was a sort of praise." His gaze met hers sheepishly. "In all sincerity, thank you for taking the time to prepare us dinner."

She grinned, feeling vindicated. "It's my pleasure. Tell me, have you always lived in Sydney?"

"Yes, originally just outside of the city on a private estate. How about you? Are you originally from Atlanta?"

"No, my stepfather's job moved us all around the country. We were in Atlanta when he retired, so I've lived there the longest. I ended up going to college there and then taking a job."

"You like it?"

She shrugged. "It's been a good place to live, but I have to admit of all the places I've been I love Sydney the best. The beauty, the people... I like everything about it."

Lucius focused on cutting a slice of tender, juicy steak. "That's nice to know. I think Kirri feels the same way about Atlanta."

"I think she'd feel that way about any place Ty was." Amanda took a bread roll.

"I guess you're right."

He sounded as if he didn't understand that kind of devotion.

They spent the rest of the meal talking about what they had done that day, the kind of music they liked, and comparing other favorite things. When they were done they carried their dishes inside and cleaned up the kitchen.

Amanda took the brownies out of the oven and turned it off. "I'll just get dessert together. I'm going to eat mine outside, so I can watch the sunset. I'd be glad to bring yours to your office."

"I can't join you?" He sounded hurt.

"Sure you can. I just thought you'd have work to do, a movie to watch… I don't want you to feel you have to entertain me."

She liked the idea of Lucius spending time with her too much.

"Would you like me to move a couple of chairs closer to the water?"

"You're starting to know me too well. That would be perfect."

Amanda pulled a couple of small plates out of the cabinet.

"I don't think it's possible to know all about you," said Lucius as he headed toward the outside door.

Amanda carried out two plates of brownie with scoops of ice cream on top and joined Lucius, who had just placed the second chair beside the first. She handed him a plate and they both sat down.

Lucius released a loud sigh of approval after

his first bite. "This may be the best dessert I've had in years."

The sound of his spoon scraping over the empty china plate came a few minutes later.

"You want some more?" she asked.

"No." His tone was regretful. "But it was delicious."

He put the plate down between them and leaned back with another sigh. She followed his lead and did the same. They said nothing as the sun, now a bright orange circle on the horizon, slowly disappeared. The only light came from the city and it didn't completely reach them.

They sat in silence for a while. And her mind was more on Lucius than the view as she finally stood up to go back inside.

His fingers were gentle as they wrapped around her wrist. "Stay a little longer. This is nice."

That was the last thing she had expected him to say. She assumed he'd want to get back to his work.

"Okay." She sat down again.

Lucius's fingers trailed across her skin and then they were gone. Amanda immediately missed their heat.

They sat there not talking for a long time, until she couldn't stand the electricity that was popping between them any longer. She wanted him to touch her. Didn't want him to touch her. He'd said it was up to her. It was a gentlemanly concept, but in reality it put all the pressure on her. Her mind said, *Don't go there!* while her disloyal body yelled, *You want him!*

Amanda stood abruptly. "I really should go in now. I need to prepare for work tomorrow. What time should I be ready in the morning?"

"Around eight will be fine." There was an unsure note in his voice, as if she had surprised him.

"I'll be ready."

She headed for her bedroom, not daring to look at Lucius for fear she would turn back and hurl herself at him.

CHAPTER SIX

THE FLASH OF lightning shook Lucius awake and the sound of thunder made him sit up. The wind swooshed around the corner of the house as fat drops of rain hit the window. He needed to get the chairs he'd left near the water secured. He should have brought them in earlier, but his mind had been filled with Amanda instead of outdoor furniture.

The wind shook the window. He shouldn't linger. The pool umbrella needed lowering as well. If he didn't move fast he'd have to fish it out of the pool in the morning. Worse, the chairs might be in the harbor and gone forever, or busted on the rocks.

Jerking on his shorts, he hurried outside through the kitchen door, flipping on a floodlight as he went.

He cranked down the umbrella, pulled it out of the center hole in the table and laid it beside the house, where it would be secure. The rain was beating down now, and rolled off his shoulders.

On bare feet he loped toward the harbor. Picking up a chair, he started toward the patio. He was halfway there when Amanda passed him, going in the other direction.

"Go inside!" he yelled over the weather.

She didn't slow down. He wasn't sure if she hadn't heard him or if she was just ignoring him. Lucius suspected the latter.

Placing the chair on the patio, he went after her. She was moving slowly across the yard struggling to carry a heavy chair. When he got to her, he took one arm of the chair and together they raced to the patio.

He glanced at Amanda. She was soaked as well. On the patio, they dropped the chair on its legs and ran for the kitchen door.

Inside, Lucius slammed the door behind them. Amanda's hair hung in rainy ropes around her face. Tiny beads of water perched on the ends of her eyelashes. Her eyes were wide and her gaze lay squarely on his chest. She licked the moisture from her lips.

He should have been chilled, standing there wet in the air-conditioning, but instead his body heated rapidly. His manhood stirred. Amanda's thin nightgown was stuck to her body, highlighting her full breasts and generous hips and leaving him in no doubt of her femininity. Her legs were long enough to circle his waist. The neon blue polish on her toes made the corner of his mouth twitch upward. Amanda was sexy in every sense of the word.

She shivered.

The movement brought him back to reality. She had less body mass than he and must be freezing.

Grabbing her hand, he said, "Come with me."

Amanda didn't argue. Another flash of lightning lit the way as he led her to his room. Her soft hiss found his ears as he pulled her through the door, but she didn't resist. Moments later they were in his bathroom. Heading straight to the shower, he opened the door and turned the water to hot.

"Strip."

She looked at him dumbfounded, not moving.

As steam built in the shower he placed his hand on her back and gave her a gentle nudge. "Get warm."

She stepped in and he closed the door.

"There'll be a towel hanging within reach out here when you're done," he called as he pulled one of the towels off the rack and began drying his hair.

Lucius glanced at the shower. He needed to get out of here. He'd made a promise, after all.

As he walked out of the bathroom he continued to dry off. Going to his dresser, Lucius pulled out a dry pair of shorts and quickly changed clothes. He needed to get Amanda back on her side of the house as soon as possible.

The bathroom door opened. Amanda stood there with the bright light as a backdrop. A towel concealed her body where she held it in place. What little he'd managed to do to ease his longing was lost in a moment. His heart thumped and his manhood grew in hard, hot desire.

Her gaze caught his and then flickered to his chest before traveling downward. Her mouth formed a small O. He could only guess that she'd seen his rigid length, which must be clearly visible behind the flimsy material of his shorts.

Amanda took a slow, hesitant step toward him that soon turned to a bolder one. She stopped just inches before she could touch him. Lucius didn't move. His breaths had turned rapid and shallow. His body tightened almost in pain with his effort not to reach for her. This must be her decision.

She rose on her toes and pressed her lips against his. One of her hands came to his shoulder, branding his bare skin. Her tongue teased his bottom lip. She nipped at it, then soothed the spot with the tip of her tongue. He opened his mouth and joined her in exploration. The kiss grew deep as she stepped closer, squeezing his hardened length between them.

Lucius wanted her badly. Had wanted her for days. Still, he needed to know she understood where this was going.

He broke the kiss and stepped back so he could see her clearly. "Just to be clear, what are you telling me, Amanda?"

Her voice was husky and very sexy as she said, "I'd have thought a man with your intelligence would know."

His look never wavered from hers. "But that doesn't mean I don't want to hear it."

She let go of the towel. "Dr. Lucius West, I want you to take me to your bed."

That was all the invitation he required.

He pulled her against him, felt her lips soft and full beneath his. Amanda met his ardor with equal abandon. Her arms circled his neck. As they tightened her breasts brushed his chest. His manhood jerked. He'd dreamed of a moment like this. Thoughts of what might happen between them had kept him awake over the last few days. Yet those imagined touches hadn't been anything like what was happening to him now. This was far more wonderful.

Her mouth opened and his tongue invaded. She tasted honey-sweet, with a nectar all her own. His hands found her waist, skimmed over her bare hips and moved down to cup her behind.

Amanda's hands moved to his shoulders. Her fingertips kneaded his skin, then traveled along his upper arm. They brushed over his ribs and down to his waist. Her hands rested there, then pulled him closer before they found the waist-band of his shorts. A finger traced the line of it before her hand slipped beneath the material. Her other hand followed suit, and moments later she'd pushed his shorts down.

His mouth left hers to place kisses along her

cheek and then nuzzle behind her ear. Amanda's soft giggle made his chest swell.

His shorts at his feet, he stepped out of them, rotated her and walked her backward to his bed. There, he turned and sat down, pulling Amanda between his legs. Her hands rested on the top of his shoulders.

Lucius looked up at her. Even with her hair mussed from where his hands had run through it she looked beautiful. Their gazes met and held. Amanda's eyes were bright with curiosity, and maybe a touch of apprehension.

"I want to admire you." Cupping her cheek, Lucius brought her lips to his.

She released a soft sigh, then kissed him in return.

His hand ran down her hips and pulled her closer before he broke contact. His attention moved to the globes of her breasts, which were full and luscious. Her nipples were extended, begging for his attention. Lifting a breast, he appreciated its weight for a moment, then kissed the curve before slipping his mouth over her tip.

Amanda rewarded him with a shiver.

"Shh…easy… You're so amazing I just want to admire you. Taste you."

He moved to the other breast, caressing it until Amanda's fingers moved through his hair and held him closer. Her groan of pleasure vibrated through him.

Then slowly her hands returned to his shoulders. She pushed him until he lay back on the bed. "It's my turn now," she said.

Lucius watched as she climbed up beside him. She ran her hands over his chest, pausing for a second to brush her palm over the hair at its center. His nerves were electrified. He caressed her from her waist to hip. Her skin was so perfect, silky-smooth.

Amanda stopped her movements and turned her attention to his lips. Using her index finger, she followed the line of his bottom lip with great care. When she did the same to the seam of his mouth he took the tip of the finger into his mouth and bit it gently. She removed it slowly before leaning down and kissing him.

Lucius joined in the heated meeting of lips, pulling her across him. The lightning flashed and the thunder rolled and the rain pounded against the window. It reminded him of the turmoil going on in his body.

He'd been aware of Amanda's passion regarding her work, even her excitement in seeing and learning new things during their sightseeing. He'd hoped those emotions would extend to the bedroom, but what she was doing to him now had gone light years beyond his most sensual dreams.

Nothing he'd shared with another woman had had him as conscious of his breathing, or the sensitivity of his skin, nor had created such an un-controllable drive in him to take her. Everything about him burned with life, all because Amanda was kissing and touching him. She had opened a door he feared he would never be able to close or would never want to.

Lucius rolled her over on the bed. He watched her eyes heat and her lips part as his palm brushed a nipple. Her look widened with anticipation as his hand traveled to her stomach and rested there before he moved it lower. Her hiss of sensual awareness rippled through him.

"One of the things I like the best about you is that I never have to guess what you like or don't like. You definitely like this…" Lucius ran his fingers between her legs once more.

"Mmm…"

"Will you open for me?"

Her legs relaxed. Seconds later he slipped his finger into her hot, wet center. Amanda lifted her hips and moaned. The sound flowed through him. His manhood throbbed. As he moved his finger in and out of her he placed kisses on her stomach, breasts and mouth.

Minutes later her back bowed and her hips rose, seconds before she shattered and whim-pered, "Lucius…"

Languidly she settled on the bed with a soft

sigh. Male satisfaction filled Lucius's chest at the look of rapture he'd placed on Amanda's face.

He watched her eyes flutter open. "I need you," he said.

A sexy invitation formed on her lips. "I'm right here."

Lucius shifted away and reached inside the bedside drawer. He removed a package. Finished covering himself, he settled over Amanda, his manhood finding her center as his lips took hers.

Her legs parted and her arms came around his neck. Lucius entered her, then pulled back. At her sound of protest he pushed forward, and pulled away again. Amanda's legs circled his hips, tightened, letting him know clearly what she wanted. He had no problem with accommodating her.

He plunged deep, filling her, and then stilled. Her heat surrounded him, held him tight, caressing him. His kiss deepened as he began to move again.

Seconds later Amanda joined him, eagerly matching his rhythm. Too soon his passion spilled, and a groan came from deep within him just as a matching cry came from her.

Lucius sank to the bed, being careful not to crush her. They remained tangled together as they caught their breath.

Something about being with Amanda seemed all too right…

* * *

Amanda slowly came out of a perfect combination of sleep and warmth. Lucius lay on his stomach with his arm thrown across her middle.

Her eyes widened. What had she done? She'd slept with Lucius! That hadn't been her best idea. Yet he'd been so tempting, standing there in the kitchen with water dripping off his head and his chest bare.

He'd caught her with her mouth still gaping when he'd pulled her into his bathroom. Her surprise had turned to shock when he had all but stuffed her into the shower. She could recognize sexual hunger in a man, and it had been written all over Lucius's face.

As she'd stood under a hot shower that had done nothing to ease the want in her she'd become angry. When she wanted something she went after it. And right then, irrational and impractical as it might be, she'd wanted Lucius. Wanted to meet his challenge.

Determined, she'd stepped out of the shower, dried her hair in a towel and walked into his room, daring him to break down that wall she'd made him erect. She still couldn't believe she'd dropped her towel and stood naked in front of the most handsome man she knew. Yet she'd found the courage to do it.

What she'd shared with Lucius had been beyond anything she'd ever had with a man before.

A generous lover, Lucius had known all the right spots to taste and touch. She'd never felt more glorious or wanted than when he'd been loving her.

She looked at him now, all strong and sensual man. Outside the storm had passed, but one grew within her and hovered like humidity on a hot day. She wanted his kisses again—and more. She needed his loving.

But she couldn't. It just wouldn't be wise. It would be too easy to want more and more from him. For as long as she could have it. And her experience told her that wouldn't be for very long.

Carefully lifting his arm, she slowly slid out from under it, then moved across the bed and off it. She headed for the door, with her own room as her intended destination.

"Where're you going?"

She jerked to a stop and turned. Lucius lay on his side with his head propped on his hand. His full attention rested on her.

"I'm going to my bed. I thought you might want to sleep by yourself."

He raised a brow. "What made you think that?"

"I don't—"

Lucius sat up and the sheet dropped to his waist leaving her with a lovely view of his chest.

"Running away, Amanda?"

She bit her upper lip. "I don't run from anything."

He waved her over. "So come back here, then."

Lucius wanted her again. It showed clearly in his eyes. But for how long? That was the crucial question, but right now that didn't seem to matter. The heat, the hunger, the promise of heaven was being offered. Just waiting for her to take it. She wouldn't let that go—yet.

His look made her bold. She strolled back to the bed. "And where exactly do you want me?"

"Right here." He patted the bed beside him.

"What if I want to be elsewhere?"

The flicker of desire in his eyes had grown to a flame as she'd walked naked toward him. She planned to stoke and stroke it into a brush fire of need.

"That's your prerogative. I'll never make you do something you don't want to."

Her heart swelled. Lucius was a good man. Too few people had a chance to see that side of him. She'd been privileged to do so, was honored he'd shared it with her.

Climbing on the bed, she straddled his hips. His eyes widened. With a smile of satisfaction she noted that Lucius's manhood had come alive. She leaned over him, holding his hands above his head as she offered her breasts to him. He sucked a nipple into his mouth. Her core clenched. He moved to the other breast, his tongue circling her nipple then licking it.

She pulled away just far enough so he couldn't reach her and looked down at him.

"Amanda…?" He watched her intently.

"Mmm…?"

"Don't tease me." Lucius's words were gruff.

She brushed against his length with her center. "Who's teasing?"

At his soft growl she smiled, then rose and slowly slipped onto his iron-hard length.

She wiggled with a sigh of satisfaction.

"Amanda!" he said, with an edge of warning.

She giggled, then lifted herself until she almost no longer held him. At his sob of complaint she completely surrounded him. She offered him her breasts once more, which he eagerly took. She rose and fell along with him as he feasted. Her insides tightened and twisted. She kissed him with desperation, wanting these sweet sensations to go on and on.

Lucius joined her in the ebb and flow of motion and soon they found their pleasure in unison.

Amanda fell forward on his chest and rested there. Lucius slowly caressed her back. She soon drifted off to sleep.

Lucius might have thought that starting a work morning with someone else around would be awkward, but with Amanda it was pleasant. He would have liked to shower with her, but he was confident that would have made them late for work. Keeping his hands off Amanda would have been impossible.

They had woken much too late anyway, and she'd hurried off to her room to dress.

He already missed her.

She'd been a lavish lover—and bold. He liked that the most about her. He shouldn't have been surprised. When she'd climbed over his hips and taken him he'd almost lost it. His wife and the women who had come after her wouldn't have dared to show their desire or what they wanted so openly.

Amanda made his life in and out of bed exciting. His days seemed a lot livelier because of her. Something he hadn't even realized he'd been missing.

But this was exactly what he'd promised himself he wouldn't let happen. Amanda was a temporary fling, just like those other women had been, but somehow, with her, it seemed different. More real.

But he'd never intended for things between them to go this far. Even if it felt like something more, he couldn't offer her anything beyond the here and now. He wasn't the guy for her long-term.

At the clinic, they both went their own ways. As much as he would have liked to kiss her, he managed to refrain.

He went about his day with a smile on his face. More than one person commented on how happy he appeared to be.

It wasn't until his secretary notified him that Amanda was there to see him that he questioned his growing feelings for her. The idea of spending time with her sent a blast of pleasure through him. And, oddly, it wasn't all to do with the idea of them being in bed together again. He liked her; it was that simple.

"Please tell her to come in," Lucius said, trying to sound cooler than he felt.

"Hey." Amanda closed the door behind her and walked toward his desk. "I just wanted to let you know that I'm moving to a hotel tonight. Staff Resources is putting me up in one. They couldn't find another apartment on such short notice, so I have to settle for a hotel."

A knot formed in the center of his chest. He'd believed she'd be staying with him again after last night. He knew it was for the best that she was moving out, but he still didn't like the plan.

"I see."

"Can you take me there this afternoon, or should I get someone else to?"

The smile he'd been wearing when she'd come in had been wiped away. Amanda was acting as if it didn't matter that she wouldn't be going home with him after work. Had last night meant so little to her?

Lucius stepped around the desk, going toward her. He took one of her hands, playing with her fingertips. "You know you're welcome at my place for as long as you wish. After all, you *do* like my house, my pool and my view. And I hope me…"

A look of sadness came over her face. "Lucius, I don't think me staying at your home is such a good idea."

"Why's that?"

"It can't end well. We don't want the same things out of life. We're literally from different sides of the world."

He wouldn't force her. She was right. Last night should remain just what it had been—a nice interlude he would remember fondly.

"I can drive you to get your belongings and then take you on to the hotel."

"Thanks, Lucius. I appreciate it."

She left without further discussion.

He stood there, trying to figure out why he didn't like anything about this arrangement. He should be pleased she was leaving his house before he became too used to her being there. In truth, he already was.

Far too soon for him, he was dropping Amanda off at the hotel. He helped her up to the room with her bag and her pillows. Carrying them around for her had fast become a habit. This time he wasn't enjoying it at all.

"Well, it isn't so bad." Amanda stood at the window. "Not the view you have, but you can't have everything."

Lucius stopped himself from saying what rested on the tip of his tongue. She was welcome to his view if she wanted it. Instead he settled for, "Have you had dinner?"

"Uh… I have a long day tomorrow, and I didn't—"

"Didn't sleep much last night," he finished flatly.

"Yes." Amanda looked at the floor, then at him. "Lucius, I want you to know that our time together was special to me, but we can't continue."

Pursing his lips, he nodded and moved toward the door. He wasn't staying around for more of those types of platitudes. Not when he wanted to take her in his arms and make her admit that last night deserved better than this casual brush-off.

"I agree."

"I'll see you around the clinic."

"I guess so."

He'd wanted short and sweet? That was exactly what he'd gotten.

He closed the door behind him. He wouldn't beg her for more. He'd begged his ex-wife to stay and he'd promised himself he'd never do that again. It had been like a kick in the teeth when she hadn't.

It was two days later when he finally saw Amanda again. He'd hungered for her. Had missed her teasing, his meals with her, even the easy silences they'd had together.

She had just presented a case study from her clinic in Atlanta. She'd been clear and precise in her presentation, answering questions without hesitation and with authority. He had been impressed with her medical knowledge and skill. Everything about her said she was a topnotch nurse, particularly her intelligence and sensitivity. All those attributes he had appreciated both in and out of bed.

Those thoughts were better kept to himself. Now that he'd had some time away from her, he understood her decision to move to the hotel had been for the best. He wasn't a good risk in the relationship department. As a husband, he'd certainly done a poor job.

As people left the room he stayed back, hoping to speak to her. He might agree with their sleeping arrangements, but that didn't mean he wasn't still drawn to Amanda.

He was speaking to someone else when she finally came up beside him. The other person left and he turned to her.

She grinned at him, and the cloud hanging over him lifted.

"I hear the 'Baby Whisperer' has struck again. Congratulations."

"What?"

"The woman you did IVF on the first week I was here has had a positive pregnancy test."

"Yes. I saw the chart. I'm pleased."

He wanted her to talk to him about something personal, but this was better than nothing. He'd so quickly gone from keeping his distance from her to needing interaction with her daily. She'd flipped his world around and he wanted it righted again.

She studied him a moment—seeing too much, he feared.

"You don't look pleased."

"I am. I *am*. We just have to be cautious, because you never know when something will go wrong. This is her third attempt. I'm being cautiously optimistic."

"She has an excellent doctor. I'm sure it'll go well. I'm sorry I won't be here to follow her case."

That's right, Amanda will be going home in a few weeks.

"I'll see that Nancy keeps you posted."

"Thank you for that."

An awkwardness settled between them as they looked at each other.

She broke the silence. "I…uh…better go. We have a delivery brewing."

Lucius nodded. But as soon as she walked away, he wanted to ask her back.

To his own surprise, he called, "Amanda?"

She turned. A small smile formed on her lips and questions filled her eyes. "Yes?"

He stepped closer, so that no one else could hear. "Would you like to have dinner with me Saturday evening? I have tickets to a jazz concert at the Opera House."

"They do jazz at the Opera House?" Amazement filled her voice.

"They do. It's a multi-purpose building."

"I learn something new every day... I'd love to go."

Would she love to because she would go to the Opera House with anyone or because *he'd* asked her? His heart jumped with happiness. It didn't matter. At least he would have a chance to spend more time with her.

"Then I'll pick you up at your hotel around seven."

"I'll be ready. I'm looking forward to it."

He was also. Far too much. Maybe he shouldn't have asked her, but he hadn't been able to help himself. If he could just spend a little more time with Amanda then possibly he would be able to get her out of his system. Surely they could spend a night out together as just friends?

With far more eagerness than he should feel he made reservations for dinner at a restaurant on the water, within walking distance of the Opera House. It had been some time since he'd been on a date and he feared his skills might be lacking.

It had been a long time since he'd tried to woo a woman…

Amanda was waiting in the hotel lobby when he arrived. Her hair had been pulled away from her face on one side. Her lips were covered in a light pink lipstick that perfectly matched the dress she wore. On her feet were pretty but sensible shoes, with bows on the top. She looked fresh, wholesome, and completely lovely.

His heart fluttered and he had to sternly remind his manhood to behave.

The tension in his chest increased as he walked toward her. A smile came to her lips. Had he just been punched in the gut? Could she be as glad to see him as he was her?

He took one of her hands in his, lightly holding her fingers. "You look splendid."

"Thank you. I didn't bring anything with me appropriate for the Opera House, so I did a little shopping this afternoon."

"You look perfect. This is for you." He handed her a single white rose. "I thought it might brighten your room. I know you have a vase."

She smelled the flower. "So nice… Do I have time to put it in water?"

He nodded. "We'll take the time."

They went up to her room and she quickly took care of the rose.

He looked around. "I don't see your pillows."

She gave him a sheepish look. "Somehow they didn't belong here."

"Are you comfortable?" It wasn't a room *he'd* want to spend weeks in.

Amanda glanced around, her lips curling. "I'm fine. Of course it doesn't have your view."

"You're always welcome at my house," Lucius added in a teasing tone, but really he wished she *would* return. The house had lost its light without her presence.

She turned her back, sitting the vase on her bedside table. Then she said, "I'm ready."

Lucius had found a parking lot that was near the restaurant and close enough for them to walk to the Opera House. He'd requested a table by the water, knowing Amanda would especially like that. He wasn't disappointed.

"Oh, this is wonderful!" She sounded awed.

He had been trying to make a good impression. She acted as if he were succeeding. "I hoped you'd like it."

She smiled. "It'll be a wonderful memory to take home."

They ate dinner, making small talk about what had happened during the week.

"I went to the ocean swimming pool this morning," Amanda announced.

"Did you see your friend the squid?"

She grinned. "I didn't—but I did keep an eye out for him."

She laughed. He loved the sound. It made him want to join her.

Finally they had worked their way back to the friendly, comfortable spot they had once had. The one he'd missed so much.

Too soon for him, it was time to leave for the concert. He hated to break the spell.

They strolled to the Opera House, not touching but staying close. As they walked up the steps to the building he took her elbow, glad for the excuse to touch her. He'd wanted to do so all night. It had been too long since he had. He'd missed the silky smoothness of her skin. Just the brief contact now reminded him of the feel of her under his hand as he ran it over her bare hip.

Shaking his head slightly, he refocused.

After they had found their places Amanda said, "These are amazing seats. Front center. When I go to a concert it's usually the back corner."

He chuckled. "It pays to be a supporter of the Opera House. First chance at tickets is a perk."

"That figures."

"You always say that about me. As if I'm a stereotype." Lucius didn't like the idea that she grouped him with other people. He wanted to stand out in Amanda's mind. Although why it mattered so much to him he had no idea.

She turned so he could see her face clearly, then placed a hand briefly on his thigh. "I can assure you that you're not a stereotype. You're a special man in ways you don't let many people see. And I'm honored because I have."

That statement was an ego-builder. Not since his father had told Lucius he'd done a good job when he'd finished first in his medical school class had he felt this good.

"Thank you."

She smiled, settled in her seat again and opened her program. "I didn't know you were a jazz aficionado."

"I think it has less to do with that and more with the fact I can get good tickets. But I do like it. My father had us listen to jazz when we were children, so I guess I picked it up. My ex-wife thought it made us look good to come to jazz concerts."

A moment went by before Amanda said, "Will you tell me about her?"

This wasn't a conversation he particularly wanted to have, yet there wasn't some big secret about what had happened between them. He'd been a lousy husband.

"We thought we were in love, only we weren't. But I guess any divorced couple can say that."

"How long were you married?"

"Three years. Three years too many, if you ask her."

"So what happened?" Amanda turned so that she faced him again.

"I was working long hours. Getting the clinic

started. Busy making a name for myself. I left her alone too much. Most of the downfall was my fault."

Amanda placed her hand on his arm. "I'm not an expert in marriage, but as I understand it, it takes two to make it work."

"Maybe so. But to hear her tell it I was more interested in seeing that other women had babies than I was in coming home to make my own. What I really think is that we just weren't suited. She was a social climber and I cared nothing for that world. I did spend a great deal of time away from her, but she didn't make it very appealing to come home."

"It sounds like you put each other out of your misery by divorcing."

"Yes, but it was still a failure on my part. One I've promised myself I'll never repeat. My work will always come first. Not just because it's important, but because it's who I am."

Silence fell and Amanda broke it. "Yet you're here with me tonight?"

Hmm, so he was. He'd have to give that some thought.

The sound of musicians tuning up turned their attention to the stage.

During the second song Amanda leaned close and whispered, "This is wonderful."

He took her hand and held it. She didn't resist. Instead she intertwined her fingers with his.

The concert ended too soon for Lucius. He could have spent hours just sitting there, holding her hand and listening to good music. That sense of wellbeing he'd never had with his ex-wife he'd found with Amanda, in so many different ways.

But what was he doing? Where was he going with this? Was he planning to ask her to marry him?

That wouldn't happen. His job demanded too much from him. Long hours at the clinic and going away to the conferences, both home and abroad, that came around frequently didn't make for a good marriage.

To become involved with him wouldn't be fair to Amanda. She probably wanted children, a family, a stable home life. He couldn't offer her that. The sense of loss left a sick feeling in his gut. Amanda deserved better than the little he could give her.

Resigned to what his future would look like, he took Amanda back to the hotel. In reality, he wanted to take her home to his bed. But he knew it had to be this way.

He walked her to the hotel elevators. Kissing her on the cheek, he said, "Goodnight."

"Thank you, Lucius, for a lovely evening."

"You're welcome. I'll see you at the clinic."

With a feeling that was pulling him down like cement shoes, he walked away.

* * *

Amanda rode up to her room, carrying a sadness as heavy as a bucket of rocks. The way Lucius had left her with such finality tore at her heart. She didn't like it. It wasn't right. Even though she'd been the one to push him away, she didn't want this canyon developing between them.

She'd take him for as long as she could have him. If that was just for a few weeks, so be it. She'd deal with her heartache when she went home. Most of her life she'd felt unwanted by one person or another, and to have Lucius want her so badly was exciting. It made her feel alive.

Before she'd even reached her floor she'd already pushed the button to go back down to the foyer.

She'd missed what they'd had together. Five mornings of waking up alone without Lucius's strong body next to her was enough. She ached to have those moments back, to share more time with him. Why be lonely when she had another choice?

There were still three more weeks before she left. Lucius still wanted her. It had been clearly showing in his eyes all night. If she could have that for just a little while longer why not grasp it? Lucius might not want her forever, but she accepted that.

She had the man behind the hotel desk call her a cab. The nearer she got to Lucius's house the more nervous she became. What if he had changed his mind about wanting her? She might live to regret this impulsive action.

The car pulled into the drive and she saw a dark house. Was Lucius not home yet? Had he already gone to bed? Had he gone out elsewhere after leaving her?

She couldn't stop now—she had to find out.

Amanda stood at the door, ready to ring the bell, and then the cab driver called out to her.

"Lady, I have another pick-up. I have to go."

With that, he left her.

She rang the doorbell, then looked down the drive.

Was the ferry still running this late at night?

There was no answer. She rang again.

Had she misjudged Lucius's signals? Those touches? Kisses? Their night together? Their evening together?

Coming here had been a mistake. She turned to leave.

Her heart jumped when the porch light flicked on and the door opened.

"Amanda?" Lucius stood there, in shorts riding low on his hips.

With a gulp, she forced the knot in her throat down. "You said I could come see your view anytime."

CHAPTER SEVEN

AMANDA BREATHED A sigh of relief and felt her blood hum through her veins as Lucius reached out and tugged her into the house.

"You should have said you were interested in my view before I left. I would've brought you home with me."

"The way I see it, you left me behind."

"Aw… Since you're here, I'll make it up to you. Come on."

His hand tightened on hers as he led her toward the back of the house.

"Why're all the lights off?"

"I was sitting outside."

Did that mean something significant?

"In the dark?"

"Yes. I was looking across the harbor, wishing you were here."

He opened the door to the patio.

Her heart went pitter-pat. He'd been missing her.

"You were?"

"I was feeling sorry for myself."

On the patio, she took the chair he offered. He pulled his own chair close before he sat. Taking her hand, he held it, gently brushing the pad of his thumb over the top of it. They stayed that way for a long time. The moment was too perfect.

Amanda looked off into the distance at the beauty of the harbor. "I've missed this view. It's so pretty."

"I feel the same way."

His tone made her look at him. Lucius watched her, not the harbor. Even in the cool air her cheeks heated at the expression in his eyes.

"I'm glad you came to join me. I've missed you."

She squeezed his hand. "You saw me just an hour ago—and at the clinic before that."

"I did, but it wasn't the same. If I could have pulled you into a closet and kissed you senseless I would have."

She giggled. "That would have been fun. The respectable Dr. Lucius West having the hots for the visiting nurse. There would've been such a scandal!"

"If you had agreed I wouldn't have cared." His voice turned raspy. "Stay with me, Amanda."

"Tonight?"

He brought her hand to his mouth, turned it over and kissed her palm. "For as long as you want."

Amanda's heart swelled. *This* was what it was like to have a man truly desire her. The fact that it was Lucius made it extra-special.

Lucius stood and led her through the kitchen

into his bedroom, stopping beside the bed. There he brought her into his arms. His kiss was slow, tender, unlike the hurried fevered ones of before. This one said, *I care about you... I have longed for you...you matter to me.*

Amanda drank in the joyous unknown feeling. She'd been searching for this connection all her life. She didn't want to fall in love with Lucius, shouldn't take a chance on her heart being broken. Yet she was halfway in love with him already. It would kill her when she had to leave, but she couldn't give up this sublime moment— or any others that might happen between them.

"This pink dress…" Lucius skimmed his hands over her waist. "It looks amazing on you, but I've thought about taking it off you all evening."

Heat pooled between her legs. She lifted her arms above her head in invitation.

Going down on a knee, Lucius placed his hands just below the hem of her dress and deliberately ran his hands up the outside of her thighs. She tingled with anticipation. He stood and finished stripping the clothing from her. He let it drop to the floor.

"Lovely…"

The word whispered across her shoulders as he pushed her bra straps away and kissed the skin beneath. Her breathing became heavy. "You say the nicest things."

He kissed the top of one of her exposed breasts as he worked the clasp of her bra open. "I'm sure that's not true. I have an entire staff that might disagree with you."

"They don't know you like I do."

Her bra joined her dress on the floor. He sighed deeply. "I have missed you. Your beauty."

Amanda shivered as his index finger caressed her breast, moved to the nipple. She reached for him, but he went down on his knee again and kissed her belly button. Looping his fingers in either side of her panties, he pushed them down.

He kissed her mound. Her fingers gripped his shoulders. "Lucius…"

He stood and lifted her against him, letting the whole length of her body glide down him. "You feel so good."

She tugged, then shoved his pants to the floor. Moving to the bed, they fell on it together. Lucius's lips found hers as they became a tangle of passion.

Sweet, satiated hours later, Lucius lay quietly in the early morning with a softly sleeping Amanda in his arms. He had been missing moments like this all his life. The darkness had disappeared with the brightness of Amanda. It couldn't last longer than a few weeks, but he'd make the most of it while he could.

Before she'd shown up on his doorstep he'd been sitting on his patio, thinking about what Amanda might be doing on the other side of the harbor. Now she lay here, in his arms.

He'd been shocked and elated when he'd opened the door and seen that she stood there. He'd tried to play it cool, not wanting to scare her off, while all he'd really wanted to do was to sweep her up into his arms and not let her go.

Rain tapped against the window. It was supposed to rain all day. He snuggled Amanda closer. He couldn't think of a better place to spend the day than in bed with her.

She wiggled against him. His manhood sprang to life.

"It's raining…" she said, more as a statement than a question.

"It is."

Amanda rolled to face him. She stroked his chest and purred, "What do you think we should do today to keep busy?"

"I was thinking of just staying right where we are."

In the past he would have never suggested such an idea. He would have gone to the clinic, made good use of his time.

"That sounds wonderful. But I do hope you mean the whole house and not just in bed, because I could use a shower and something to eat."

He kissed her. "I think that can be arranged. You shower with me and I'll help with breakfast."

"I'm going to need to get my clothes from the hotel."

He fondled her breast, making the nipple stand to attention. "You won't need them today. We'll get up early tomorrow morning and stop by the hotel on our way to the clinic. I miss those pillows."

She giggled and ran her hand over his growing manhood. "Sounds like a plan."

Amanda smiled as she watched Lucius do another lap of the pool. These last few days had been pure bliss.

The routine had been easy to get used to. Their days started with her waking up in Lucius's bed. His arms were always around her, as if he had pulled her to him in his sleep. More often than not they shared a shower before eating breakfast together, and then Lucius drove them to work.

He would give her a quick kiss before exiting the car. They weren't trying to keep their relationship a secret, but they weren't advertising it either.

Occasionally their paths crossed at the clinic. Lucius would give her a heated look that promised something wonderful that evening. And more than once he'd caught her staring at him during a meeting. With each of those interactions she'd left with a tingle of eagerness for more time alone with him.

She'd never felt more desired, more appreciated.

In her experience, men didn't want her. Her father, as irrational as it was, had made her feel unwanted because he'd died. Her stepfather had made it clear she wasn't welcome because she damaged his perfect family picture. Then there had been her boyfriends, who had left her because they hadn't been able to handle her being so driven. The worst had been her last boyfriend, who had destroyed her by making her believe he'd actually loved her.

Being with Lucius had wiped all those negative feelings away and replaced them with precious ones.

She remained painfully aware that what they had wouldn't last. But a girl could dream, couldn't she? And the idea of that dream was sweet enough that she could accept the consequences of a reality without Lucius.

She'd just have to live on the memories. With this staff exchange on her résumé she would focus on her career and try to put her hopes and dreams of more into a box in her mind, bringing the memories out on days when she felt less than wanted.

The first part of the week at the clinic had been slower than usual, with only one baby delivery.

Neither she nor Lucius had been needed after-hours.

When she joined him in the car at the end of each day he would immediately grab her hand and pull her to him for a kiss.

The feeling of being the focus of his desire was heady. He acted as if he couldn't get enough of her. After a lifetime of not being enough, or feeling as if she stood on the outside watching a play she'd never be a part of, she felt as if she'd found heaven.

Each evening Lucius would offer to take her to dinner but she always declined, wanting to cook a simple meal for them, eat on the patio with him and hold hands as the sun went down. Then, best of all, she would go to bed with Lucius. There, he was a generous and attentive lover. Her satisfaction seemed as important to him as his own and he never failed to make her feel desired.

On Thursday morning Dr. Johannsson stepped into the room where Amanda had just finished seeing a patient.

"Amanda, I think you might like to attend the examination of my next patient. It's an out of the ordinary case. It's also one we'll be discussing this afternoon during the patient conference."

"That sounds intriguing."

She followed the doctor to the exam room down the hall. Outside of it, Dr. Johannsson stopped.

"This is a forty-year-old woman who is borderline hypertensive and who had an ectopic pregnancy after the last IVF done by Dr. West a year ago. She presented with mild ovarian hyperstimulation syndrome, but that cleared up in six days. She's here requesting to be considered for IVF again."

"How early did the OHSS start?" Amanda asked.

"During the second round of shots."

Amanda nodded. This woman didn't sound like a great candidate for another course of IVF.

Dr. Johannsson's lips pursed. "To complicate the matters further, she has an inverted uterus."

This was indeed a case worth paying attention to.

She and Dr. Johannsson entered the room. On the examination table waited a woman with faultless make-up and hair. Everything about her said she came from an affluent background. A man in business attire stood beside her.

"Hello, Mrs. Moore… Mr. Moore. It's nice to see you." Dr. Johannsson moved toward the couple. "I'd like for you to meet Amanda Longstreet. She's a nurse visiting from America."

Amanda nodded. "It's nice to meet you both."

"Amanda is going to see to your vitals, Mrs. Moore," Dr. Johannsson said, before she started asking both the Moores some questions.

Removing the stethoscope from her neck, Amanda listened to the woman's heart-rate and respirations. All sounded well. She went on to check her pulse points, then her blood pressure. It registered in the high normal range.

Mr. Moore left the room and Dr. Johannsson pulled on plastic gloves and took a seat on the stool at the end of the exam table. "Now, let's see how you're doing."

Amanda assisted as the doctor went about her examination.

Soon she pushed back. "Mrs. Moore, I'd like Nurse Longstreet to examine you as well. Will that be okay?"

The woman nodded.

Pulling on gloves, Amanda took her position. Finished, she stood and removed her gloves. "Mrs. Moore, would you mind if I pushed on your abdomen? It won't take but a moment."

"That's fine," the woman agreed.

Amanda started palpating the area below her belly button. "Please let me know if it hurts anywhere. I understand you've had some pain in the past?"

"Yes."

Amanda stepped back so that she could see Mrs. Moore's face. "How about now?"

"I'm doing okay."

"Good. Thank you for letting me examine you." Amanda smiled at the woman.

Dr. Johannsson said, "You may sit up now, Mrs. Moore. I'll look over your lab work and test results and get back to you soon. It has been good to see you again."

Back in the hall, Dr. Johannsson turned to Amanda. "Amanda, would you mind presenting this case at the patient conference this afternoon? I've had something come up."

"I'll be glad to."

Amanda's second thought was she would be doing so in front of Lucius. It mattered to her that he be proud of her.

Lucius took the last seat on the front row, facing the screen in the conference room, which was arranged in theater-style. The patient meeting had already been called to order. He looked around the room for Amanda. He located her on the right side, one row up. She sat with a group of Labor and Delivery nurses.

The best he could tell, from what had been said and the actions of other staff members when she was around, Amanda had meshed with the rest of the team as if she had been there for years. They not only seemed to like her, but they admired her work ethic and her knowledge. She would be an asset to the clinic if she decided to stay.

The idea sent excitement through him. But that wasn't something he and Amanda had discussed or the clinic had offered. She had long-term plans at her clinic in Atlanta, didn't she? What made him think she'd even consider staying in Sydney?

He looked at her for long enough that she turned and met his gaze. Lucius smiled and she returned it. It was empowering to have a woman show openly how she felt about him. He appreciated the unfamiliar feeling...treasured it.

Over the last few weeks his life had changed drastically for the better—because of her. He'd started to appreciate his life outside of the clinic. Everything no longer revolved around his work. He now looked forward to going home. There was someone to share it with him. And in a strange, unexpected way, it made coming to work nicer too. He had even started keeping regular hours.

He had been lonely. Before Amanda he would never have admitted that. Now he could see it clearly.

He was very conscious of the fact she would return to America soon. That remained his emotional safety net. He surely couldn't mess things up in such a short time? He could be what she needed for at least a few more weeks, couldn't he? He'd not done well in his marriage, but that had been over a much longer amount of time. Whatever this was, he was glad he had it with Amanda.

The colleague who was running the meeting stood and announced, "Amanda Longstreet will be presenting for Dr. Johannsson today."

Amanda stepped forward and took the clicker from him. A slide appeared on the screen with medical data and Amanda started to speak. "This is Mrs. Moore. Dr. Johannsson and I saw her today in the clinic..."

She went on to share the history of the patient.

He loved her voice. The slow enunciation of her words and her dropping of letters he found delightful. In truth, he couldn't get enough of it—especially when she drew out his name when she reached her climax. Even as she stood now, in front of a group of people, speaking with authority and familiarity on her subject, he still loved the cadence of her speech.

He glanced around to find everyone's attention on her. Amanda had a way about her that made people listen attentively.

"Today, after a thorough examination, I found scarring on her vaginal wall and also a golf-ball-sized fibroid. It's Dr. Johannsson's recommendation that Mrs. Moore not be considered for further IVF."

Lucius sat straighter. He'd done Mrs. Moore's first IVF. "I don't agree," he said.

Amanda turned to face him and he saw she had that look on her face. The one she'd worn when she'd dug in about his patient during her first week there.

"Why's that?" Amanda demanded.

He sat forward. "I've had success with a new procedure that she would be a prime candidate for."

Amanda frowned. "Despite the fact she had OHSS?"

"That was a mild case. There's no reason to suspect that will happen again."

The other staff members around them faded away. The room had come down to him and her.

"And the ectopic pregnancy?"

He came back with, "That's not unusual in the practice of IVF."

"Agreed—but she lost three babies before coming to us."

Lucius liked her statement of ownership about the clinic, but he still couldn't agree with her about the case.

"There's also the issue of her inverted uterus," she added.

Lucius leaned back in his chair, crossing his arms over his chest. "We deal with those all the time too."

"Yes, but not along with all the other negatives going against her. Based on the normal guidelines, she isn't a good candidate." Amanda glared at him.

Judging by the thinness of her lips, she had worked herself up to feeling angry.

"She is just the kind of woman we should be helping," he continued in an even tone. "Women come to us for the opportunity to have a baby. We should offer that whenever we can. And I believe I have the skills to do it."

"I'm not questioning that. What I do know is Labor and Delivery. A woman who has already had issues has a much higher chance of losing her baby and experiencing difficulties during delivery. It isn't just about implanting a baby, but carrying it to term, and a healthy birth, and having a healthy mother afterward. There are protocols in place for a reason. At my clinic in Atlanta Mrs. Moore would *not* be a good candidate and would be told so."

Lucius took a moment before he spoke. "Based on my scientific knowledge and experience, I still believe she can be helped."

"I disagree." Amanda's tone held a stinging note. "Emotional and financial well-being are important as well. Sometimes saying no is being compassionate. It isn't always about furthering medical success."

Lucius flinched. She might as well have said he was only interested in promoting his own success.

Her words hung in the air between them. An audible sound of surprise echoed around the room. She'd dared to contradict him in front of other medical staff.

Was he really that dogmatic in his beliefs and actions? Until that moment he'd have said he was unquestionably focused on the whole patient. Maybe some of his ego had been involved—or at least his drive to wipe out infertility might make it look so. But was that realistic?

Whichever it was, Amanda had made him step back and think.

The doctor in charge of the meeting came to stand beside Amanda. The room came alive again.

"I'm sure Dr. Johannsson will have further data on this issue. We'll revisit this patient next week."

When the meeting broke up a group of nurses surrounded Amanda. Lucius overheard one of them say, "I can't believe you talked to Dr. West that way. *No one* does that."

He couldn't hear Amanda's response, but he would have liked to. Did his staff really think he was that inflexible?

Lucius left before speaking to Amanda and headed for his office. What was his evening with her going to be like after that heated discussion?

An hour later, as he walked toward the car, he received a text from Amanda. She had to stay late for a delivery. She told him she would get a taxi home. He offered to come get her, but she insisted it wouldn't be necessary.

Lucius drove out of the parking lot, restless at not having Amanda with him.

He didn't like thinking she might be angry with him. At the end of his marriage his wife had been mad at him more times than not. It had soon begun not to matter to him. But the idea that Amanda was unhappy because of him caused him worry. Which surprised him. It had snuck up on him how important she had become.

With Amanda not home, he had a sandwich for dinner, did some laps in the pool, and then chose to watch TV in the living room. His bedroom wasn't very inviting without Amanda there. He had it bad.

Sometime in the night he heard the door to the bedroom across the house close softly. The shower came on. Maybe she didn't want to wake him by taking a shower in his bathroom. He went to his bed and waited, giving her a few minutes to join him.

Fifteen minutes went by and Amanda didn't show.

Concerned about her, and equally worried that she might still be angry with him, Lucius crossed the house. He opened the door to the bedroom to find Amanda in bed, already asleep. She probably hadn't wanted to wake him. She must be exhausted.

He eased into bed beside her. Amanda opened her eyes and snuggled against him.

"I thought you'd want me to sleep over here since I disagreed with you in public today," she murmured.

"No disagreement will ever make me not want you in my bed."

Had she been sent to her room as a child, when

she'd disagreed with her stepfather? What made her think he wouldn't want her?

"I like the sound of that."

She settled close with a sigh, and soon her breathing evened out into sleep again.

Amanda woke still snuggled against Lucius's chest. She didn't like fighting with him. She'd been disappointed that they hadn't agreed on the case, but she appreciated that they were each their own person. At least he hadn't demeaned her, or shot down her point of view—instead he'd offered his own calmly and methodically.

"Hey..." Lucius's fingers started caressing her hip.

She smiled. "Hey, yourself. You look mighty serious for so early in the morning."

"I don't like fighting with you."

He'd told her he and his wife had done it often. She didn't want any of that in their relationship.

"I don't like fighting with you either. Not to start another one, but I just want you to know I do believe in your skills." She grinned at him. "I also know the 'Baby Whisperer' can't possibly help everyone."

"I don't like that term. What I do, science backs up. I'm just a doctor looking for a way to help as many people as I can."

She cupped his face. "I realize that. You're humbler than people know, and you have integrity, but with our jobs there comes a certain amount of pride as well. I think sometimes you get too wrapped up in the idea you must help every woman have a baby. That's a byproduct of your big heart."

"In there somewhere was a compliment—I'm sure of it. I'd hate to debate with you all the time."

Amanda grinned. "I'll tell you what—why don't we agree to disagree, and celebrate when we do agree?"

"Especially when it's after business hours. I don't like fighting with you. But I sure would enjoy making up." He moved to kiss her.

She stopped him with a push against his chest, before running for the bathroom.

"Are you okay?" Lucius called from the bed.

"I must've eaten something that didn't agree with me last night. We had some food brought in. I'm allergic to spinach—there must have been some in the dip."

She heaved again.

"What can I do to help you?" Lucius stood at the door, concern clear on his face.

"I'll be fine."

She was holding her stomach.

"I think you should stay home today. You're pale. And if you do have something contagious we don't need you spreading it. A good rest over the weekend should be the ticket."

She leaned over the toilet once more.

Lucius pulled a washcloth from the cabinet, wet it and placed it over her forehead. He held it there while she retched again. Afterward, he gently wiped her face and mouth.

He helped her to stand on weak knees. Then put a hand on her back and steadied her as she returned to bed. He tucked her in.

"You sleep. I'll give the clinic a call to let them know we both won't be coming in today."

"Aren't you afraid they'll ask questions? I thought we didn't want anyone to know."

Rather gruffly he said, "I don't care who knows I'm seeing you."

"Thanks for taking care of me."

He gave her a kiss on the forehead. "I'll get crackers and some tea for you."

She tugged on his fingers as he started to leave her. "When was the last time you called in and said you weren't coming to work?"

He looked down at her. "Not ever that I remember."

Amanda's heart swelled with tenderness for him. "That was my guess. We'll be the talk of the clinic!"

Lucius couldn't have been more attentive the entire day. He'd even gone out to a café when she'd said she believed she might eat some chicken noodle soup. She'd wanted to go to the table in the kitchen to eat, but he'd insisted he would bring her a tray. They had shared the simple meal in her bed.

Late in the afternoon, she woke from a nap to find Lucius reading in a chair nearby.

"You do know I'm not dying? In fact, I feel much better."

"I'm glad you do, but it hasn't hurt for you to take it easy for a day."

"Maybe not—but I'm certainly not used to doing so. What I'd like to do right now is cuddle up next to you and watch a good movie. I'll even let you pick one out if you want to."

"How very generous of you, since you usually have a strong opinion on what we should view." He came to lie beside her with his head propped on his hand, a smile on his face.

"So what you're saying is that you don't care for a woman with an opinion?"

He brushed a lock of hair off her cheek. "I actually appreciate all your opinions."

"Except when I disagree with you—like yesterday?"

He picked up her hand. "Let's not revisit that. We've already made an agreement which I plan to honor."

That evening she encouraged him to go for a swim, so he'd stop hovering. It was sweet, but she felt fine now. And on Saturday Amanda felt well enough to take a walk around the neighborhood in the afternoon, although that morning she'd been under the weather again—but not sick enough to run for the bathroom.

As they walked Lucius held her hand. More than once he was the first to speak to the people they passed.

That evening he prepared dinner, insisting that she hadn't recovered enough to be "messing around in the kitchen". He proudly produced macaroni and cheese and sliced tomato. She sat watching him, enjoying the capable movements she recognized from seeing him at work in the clinic.

He truly was an amazing man. She would miss him desperately when she left.

On Sunday she still wasn't feeling a hundred percent, but she dealt with it. Despite being cooped up at the house most of the time, she found the time had flown by. She couldn't seem to get enough of Lucius. Having him all to herself was intoxicating. She had a driving need to soak up as much of him as she could, while she still had the opportunity.

That afternoon, Lucius said, "I'd like to take you somewhere special next weekend."

His fingers played with hers as they lounged next to each other after a swim in the pool.

"That sounds like fun. Where will we go?"

"I want it to be a surprise."

The words were said almost as if he were thinking out loud.

"That sounds interesting. Any place will be great since I haven't seen much but the city."

"Then I'll make arrangements. Would you prefer to leave after work on Friday or early Saturday morning?"

"I can be ready to go on Friday. Now you have my curiosity up."

She rolled toward him and moved across the small space between them. She ran her leg up his, caressing him as she snuggled close, kissing his neck.

"Is there any chance that I can convince you to tell me where we're going?"

He chuckled, bringing his arm around her and pulling her across his chest. "I don't think so, but I do like the idea of you trying."

CHAPTER EIGHT

LUCIUS DIDN'T KNOW when he had laughed more than he had during the last week. Amanda had taken finding out where they were going as a full-scale mission that would rival any military maneuver. He'd endured questions like, "What clothes should I pack?" "Will it be hot or cold?" "How far away are we going?" "Are we driving or flying?" "Do I need an evening dress?"

To everything he had simply answered yes.

As her frustration rose and his determination to surprise her became firmer, she turned to trying to get her own way in bed. They'd had sex in ways he'd only dreamed of. To say he was a thoroughly satisfied man would be an understatement.

She'd even stooped to teasing him at work.

And then one day during lunch, late in the week, she came to his office and locked the door behind her.

He looked up from behind his desk. "Amanda? Is something wrong?"

"Yeah, I want to talk to you."

"Is there a problem?" He pushed back from the desk.

She came toward him with a look of purpose on her face. "Yes, there is."

His concern built and he stood up. "Is someone hurt?"

"Someone is *going* to be hurt." She circled the desk.

"I'm not following you." He was truly confused now.

"You'll need to sit down for this."

She gave him a light shove in the center of his chest with her palm. Placing her hands on the arms of his chair, she leaned in, her nose almost touching his.

"Don't you think there's something you should tell me?"

Lucius grinned. He understood now.

"I don't know of anything…"

A smile still on his face, he looked away from her, as if giving it a lot of thought.

She kissed him. It was deep, wet and hot—and best of all it was endless.

He went rock-hard instantly. The woman was going to kill him—worse, make him useless to anyone but her.

Amanda straddled him, her center firmly against his throbbing need as she continued to kiss him until he was mindless.

"Is there something you want to tell me *now*?"

And make this heaven stop? "No…"

She stood up then, glaring at him with a teasing twist to her lips. "Ooh, you make me so mad."

He grabbed her around the waist and pulled her

back to him. "Oh, no, you don't. You can't come in here, teasing me, and then think you can just leave me like this."

He pushed at her elastic-waisted scrub pants.

"Lucius, we can't. This is your office."

But despite her half-hearted protest she'd already stepped out of her clogs and pants.

"So..."

He touched her heated valley, slipped a finger into her wet center. A soft *"Oh..."* fell from her lips before she closed her eyes and her head fell back. A few minutes later, when her knees buckled, he brought her up to him, kissing her to keep her from screaming.

He whispered against her ear. "Undo my pants, Amanda, I need to be inside you."

Her hands shook but she managed to do as he'd requested. He didn't have to tell her what to do next. She straddled him, sliding down until she'd taken all of him.

If someone had asked him what paradise was he'd have said that moment. All too soon finished.

He sat there still inside her for a while. It felt almost as wonderful as what they had just been doing.

The ring of his desk phone brought them back to reality. Amanda started to move but he held her in place.

He picked up the phone. "Yes?"

"They're waiting on you in the IVF room,"

his secretary said, with a note of curiosity in her voice.

"Tell them I'm on my way." He hung up.

Amanda buried her face in his shoulder. "She knows…"

Lucius chuckled.

Amanda gave him a slap to the shoulder. "It's not funny."

"Maybe not. But it's not like we don't talk about sex around here regularly. We could tell her we were conducting an experiment."

Amanda smirked, then scooted off his lap and turned to pick up her pants. He ran his palm across her behind. She slapped it away. He grinned, closing his pants as he watched her finish gathering her things.

"How am I going to face her?" Her cheeks were a bright pink.

He took her by the shoulders. "Honey, settle down. If it'll make you happy I'll send her on an errand, then you can slip away."

"You'd do that?"

"I'd do anything for you."

That made him pause for a moment, a little shaken. He found he truly meant it.

"Give me time to get to the IVF room, then I'll call her and have her bring me a file. You go on into the bathroom and get yourself cleaned up." He gave her a quick kiss.

She clutched her clothes to her and headed for the bathroom off his office.

"By the way—you're welcome in my office anytime."

Her eyes twinkled at him. "I might come back if you tell me where we're going on the weekend."

Lucius barked a laugh and opened the door. His secretary wore a knowing smile but he didn't care one bit. He was happy.

Amanda looked forward to Friday with gladness and sadness. Gladness because she and Lucius would be leaving for some place unknown, and sadness because she'd enjoyed their week of teasing—especially their time in his office. It had been embarrassing, seeing the meaningful smiles she'd received afterward, but so worth it.

She woke Friday morning with another queasy stomach, but it soon passed. She hadn't eaten much the night before, and she put it down to being hungry. She soon pushed it aside in her excitement over the coming weekend.

After much pleading she had gotten out of Lucius just enough to know she should take a nice dress, a swimsuit and some casual clothes. Which wasn't much different from what she would have packed if he had told her nothing.

He could be such a stubborn man.

She almost danced into the clinic. No one had

ever taken the time or cared enough to surprise her with anything. Her mother might have wanted to, but her stepfather would have never allowed it. None of her boyfriends had ever tried.

Lucius made her feel special and she would appreciate all that she could get with him. The hours until they left couldn't pass fast enough for her.

After she'd seen her last patient, she all but ran to Lucius's car. He'd texted that he would meet her there. She swung open the door and hopped in, giving him a quick kiss.

He grinned back at her. "You ready?"

"Yes. Are you going to tell me where we're going *now*?" She buckled herself in.

"Nope."

"Aw, come on Lucius. I'll know when we get there."

"Then you can wait."

He drove out of the parking lot.

"You're so mean."

She knew she sounded like a child on Christmas Eve, who wasn't allowed to open her present until the next day.

"That's not what you were saying last night." He gave her a mischievous grin.

She huffed, crossed her arms across her chest and looked out the window. She liked this laid-back Lucius. To think she'd once thought of him as a stuffed shirt...

The next thing she knew the car had stopped

and it had turned dark. Lucius stood outside, talking to a blue-vested uniformed porter. The man was busy removing their luggage from the trunk of the car.

Lucius opened her door. "Hey—you want to get out and see where we are?"

"You're *so* funny."

He grinned. She loved his happy face.

"I was beginning to wonder if you even cared, since you slept all the way here."

That was another thing that was odd about the way she felt. She was more sleepy than usual…

"Where are we?"

"The Central Coast Resort."

He said it as if that would explain everything to her.

She looked around. The building was a low modern one, nestled among lush greenery. Everything about it, from the opulent orange flowers in the lobby to the elegant woman behind the reception desk, screamed luxury. The wide lobby had been decorated in contemporary furnishings and a blue color scheme.

She and Lucius were escorted to a bungalow, where their luggage had already been placed. It consisted of a spacious living area, a bedroom through a door to the right, and a patio that looked out toward the ocean. Amanda couldn't see it, but she could hear the soothing sound of waves rolling in.

After their escort had left, Lucius turned to her. "I thought we'd just eat dinner here, since it's so late."

"That sounds nice." She looked back at him from the patio door. "Lucius, this place is amazing."

"I hoped you'd like it. A number of my acquaintances have mentioned they've been here and said I should come."

She smiled. He hadn't brought a woman here before. That made the visit extra-special for her. And yet it also remained another reminder that they came from different worlds. Never could she afford to stay in a place like this. And she certainly hadn't been raised with this type of extravagance.

Their dinner was a quiet affair on the patio. Despite her nap, Amanda was looking forward to bed. She requested that they leave the doors open, so she could hear the waves. Their lovemaking that night—and for her that was what it had become—was slow and tender. Even Lucius seemed to want it to go on forever.

Saturday morning, she woke and stretched wide across the bed. Lucius stood at the patio door with a cup of coffee in his hand. She took a few moments to admire his broad back, his slim hips and solid legs. This would be a memory she would hold close.

He turned. "How long have you been awake?"

"Long enough to enjoy the view." She smiled.

He walked toward her. "You're always trying to be funny."

"Trying? I'm insulted. I think I'm always *being* funny." She let the sheet drop just enough to show one breast.

He came to her side of the bed, within touching distance. "So, what would you like to do today?"

"I was thinking I'd like to take a long walk on the beach with you and then come back and attack your body." She ran her fingers down his arm.

"Now, *that* sounds like a plan. How about a couple's massage after that?"

Amanda stretched sinuously. Lucius's eyes flamed, his focus clearly on her breasts that were now fully exposed. She smiled again.

Lucius deliberately set his coffee cup down on the bedside table. His hands went to either side of her hips as he leant over her. Her heartbeat revved up, as it did every time Lucius looked at her with desire.

"But I think we'll change up the plan a little… Bed first, walk second."

She giggled. "Do you intend to feed me somewhere in this plan?"

"I can…" Lucius's lips found hers.

Amanda welcomed him with open arms.

The day was turning out more splendidly than she could have imagined.

* * *

At a knock on the door, Lucius climbed out of bed, quickly pulled on shorts and soon returned with a push-tray loaded with toast, fruit and cheese, along with tea and coffee. Again they ate at the table on the patio.

"This is wonderful. The view is almost as nice as yours. You're spoiling me."

He looked pleased with himself. "That was my intention."

"You keep this up and I'll never leave."

Why had she said that? She'd promised herself she wouldn't think about anything but the here and now.

"About that... Have you ever thought of staying here? Working at the clinic? We don't have openings often, but we could always make room for someone with your skills."

Lucius wanted her to stay for her nursing abilities? He didn't want her to stay for him? That hurt. Took the edge off her happiness.

"I already have a good position in Atlanta. There's one position coming open soon that I've been working for years to be qualified for. With this exchange, I should be considered."

"Maybe we can rework things at the clinic so that you could have a position equal to it—or even better."

Still he wasn't offering himself as part of

the deal. "What are you really asking?" she de-manded.

He sighed. "I'm going to miss you."

She laid her hand over his, resting on the table. "And I'm going to miss you more than I can say. Maybe we'll see each other at a conference some-time. The world is a small place in our field."

"I'd like that."

"I would too."

Sadly, she didn't think that would happen. But right now, her attention should be directed at soaking up as much of Lucius as she could.

Lucius was all too aware of the fact that Amanda would be leaving soon. It clouded his thoughts—especially when he wasn't with her. He'd brought her to the resort so they could focus on each other, not to think about the clinic, their patients or being called away. He refused to let their con-versation earlier in the day put a damper on the rest of their time together this weekend.

He'd offered her a job hoping it would entice her to stay in Sydney. Something was telling him she wanted to stay and his gut feeling was rarely wrong.

So why wouldn't Amanda consider a job with him?

They could continue what they had started and see it out to the end. Maybe they would come out on the other side as good friends who had done some remarkable medical work together.

Or could they work out a geographical compromise? But they couldn't live further apart, and right now, it appeared an impossibility. He had his work here and she had her dreams elsewhere.

Why couldn't he be one of those?

Other than that one issue over a patient, he and Amanda were highly compatible. They certainly were in bed. But what if he couldn't sustain a good relationship with her outside of bed? His risk of failure was too great to jeopardize Amanda's happiness. For right now, he must just concentrate on having her remember him with happiness.

They'd gone to the spa for their massages. Having one wasn't his usual idea of time well spent, but he'd enjoyed his mostly because Amanda had been near. The smile on her face afterward had been worth the effort. He'd also made arrangements for her to have a facial, and her fingernails and toes done.

When she'd claimed he'd already spent too much on her, he'd pulled her into a hug. "You work hard and you deserve for someone to do something nice for you. I can do that."

Amanda had gazed at him as if he'd just told the moon to move out of its orbit for her.

"We'll dine out tonight," he said now. "Wear

your pink dress—or go to the boutique and get something new. Charge it to the bungalow."

She all but glowed with pleasure.

This was what it felt like to please a woman. He'd spent years not making his sister or his ex-wife happy. It was self-confidence-building to know he pleased Amanda.

They were dressed for dinner and ready to leave their bungalow later when he pulled out the box that held a bracelet with pink diamonds all the way around it. He was worried that it might send the wrong message, but when he'd seen it, it had reminded him of Amanda. Confident that her practical side wouldn't allow her to buy a new dress, and she would be wearing the pink one for their dinner, he'd bought the bracelet.

"I have something for you."

"Lucius, I don't need anything more. Today has been wonderful. I've never been more pampered." She waved her newly painted nails.

"I saw this and thought of you." He opened the box.

She gasped. "Oh, Lucius, it's beautiful. You shouldn't have."

"Why not?"

She really didn't expect him to do nice things for her. The women he'd had experience with had all but demanded it.

"Because I don't usually go anywhere I'd

wear something so fine." She lightly fingered the stones.

"I'll tell you what—wear it tonight, and if you don't want it after that I'll return it."

She kissed him. "It's not that I don't want it. It's lovely. No one has ever given me something so splendid. But because of that I'm doing a poor job of being grateful."

He brought her near him again and kissed her. "I promise it isn't too nice for you."

Her eyes sparkled with moisture, and he came close to telling her they would be staying here in the bungalow for the evening—but this weekend wasn't about him.

They had their meal at one of the restaurants at the resort. Lucius noticed that Amanda touched the bracelet a few times. Her liking his choice made something around the area of his heart glow.

After dinner, they danced. He was so out of practice his efforts reminded him of when he'd been an adolescent at a mandatory dance and he'd have rather have been in his dorm room reading. But Amanda encouraged him. Being with her made almost anything easier.

By the time they returned to the bungalow it had started raining. It was a slow and steady fall.

Amanda opened the door to the patio. "I love the sound of rain."

She started to close it but he said, "Leave it."

Then he lit a candle at the bedside and went to stand behind her, wrapping his arms around her.

She snuggled back against him. They stood like that for a long time, both deep in their own thoughts. Finally he undressed her, except for the bracelet, and carried her to bed. Their gazes held as he removed his own clothing.

He made slow love to her by the light of the flickering flame and to the sound of gentle rain.

They spent another lazy morning together the next day. And after eating a late breakfast they headed back toward Sydney. Just outside of Mardi, Lucius turned off the main road.

Amanda perked up in her seat. "Where're we going?"

"You'll see."

"Is this another one of your surprises?" She gave him a pointed look.

He smiled as she touched her bracelet again. "I think you'll like this one the best."

"I don't think that's possible. The weekend has already been perfect. *You've* been perfect." She ran her hand down his thigh.

He clasped her hand and brought it to his mouth for a kiss.

Soon he turned at a sign that read "Billabong Park."

"Are we going to a zoo?" Amanda leaned forward, searching out the window. She almost hummed with excitement.

"We are. I thought you'd like to see some of our native animals. And the nice thing about this zoo is that many of the animals roam free, so you can touch them."

"This is so exciting!"

Lucius wasn't sure it was. He hadn't been to a zoo in years. Since he was a child. Even then it had been with a school group.

They held hands as they strolled along the paved walkways. They saw birds, crocodiles, kangaroos—and snakes. Amanda didn't want to spend much time with them, and that was fine with him. He'd saved the best for last.

"We need to go right up here." He led her toward a small shed.

"Why? I don't think there is anything up this way." Amanda searched the area.

"Trust me."

She squeezed his hand. "Always."

The word seemed to hold more weight than just her trusting in what direction he was taking her in.

As they reached the small building a woman wearing the park's uniform stepped out, holding a koala bear.

"Look! A koala! Isn't he cute?"

"Would you like to hold him?" the woman asked.

"*Can* I?" Amanda looked at Lucius.

"Sure you can. Didn't you say that day at the

beach party that you wanted to hold a koala bear?"

"You remembered?" She seemed surprised.

"I remember everything about you."

She beamed at him. "I think that's the nicest thing anyone has ever said to me."

Amanda had managed to embarrass him, and he didn't embarrass easily.

"Go on and hold the animal."

Walking over to the woman, Amanda took the koala in her hands. It perched on her arm, with its head above her shoulder. Amanda's smile went from ear to ear. She spoke quietly to the animal, petting it softly.

It took Lucius a moment to realize his smile had grown as broad as Amanda's. He was enjoying her joy.

He knew that people believed he didn't smile enough. Kirri especially complained about it. What would she think if she saw him now? He probably looked like a clown...

Amanda carefully handed the animal back to the zoo worker and re-joined him. She wrapped her hand around one of his forearms, came up on her toes and kissed him on the cheek.

"You brought me here just for that. Thank you."

This woman had him wrapped around her little finger. He knew he'd never be the same again. It would take him a long time to recover from Amanda.

He kissed her forehead. "The zoo was on our way home."

"Say what you want, Dr. West, but I know you're one special guy."

They arrived home just before dark. And as Lucius prepared for bed his phone rang. The nurse on the phone told him he was needed at the clinic. He hated to leave Amanda but they were already back to reality. And for him that meant his work.

"Amanda?"

"In here," she called from the bathroom.

"I need to go check on something at the clinic. I won't be long."

"Do you need my help?" She put her arm around his waist as they walked to the front door.

"No. I'll be back soon." He gave her a quick kiss and hurried to the car.

As he drove out of the drive Amanda stood on the front porch. He knew she would be waiting for him to return. Yeah, it would be difficult when she left.

Five days, six hours, and forty-two minutes from now...

Amanda woke to feel a flipping sensation in her stomach. Her hand pressed on her middle. A question had been niggling at her. The answer lay just beyond what she wanted to believe, to accept.

It couldn't be morning sickness.

Why couldn't it? She and Lucius had certainly made love often enough.

But they'd used protection.

She groaned. They'd missed a few times when the heat of the moment had overcome them—including that very first night they'd spent together. Still, she couldn't accept it.

Yet she hadn't been herself for over a week. Feeling unwell from eating something bad wouldn't have gone on this long. And she would've recovered from a virus by now as well.

It was time she faced reality. Reality being she needed to take a pregnancy test.

She'd anticipated it would be easy to do so in a fertility clinic, but it turned out to be more complicated than she'd have believed. The clinic had been particularly busy for a Monday, and she hadn't been able to find a time when she was alone in the supply room to pick up a test, or a moment long enough for her to get away unnoticed.

She couldn't afford any speculation about what she was doing. Even though it had become pretty much common knowledge that she and Lucius were seeing each other.

When the word had gotten out they had both taken some good-natured teasing, but that had soon died down. Even with this acceptance of their relationship Lucius deserved to know before anyone else if she was pregnant. That was if the test came back positive. She still wasn't confident that it would.

She'd administered hundreds of these tests during her career. None had been this hard to manage. Could it be because this one was the first she'd ever done on herself?

During lunch she went to the supply room, acting like a secret agent on an assignment. There she pulled a test out of the plastic box where they were stored, stuffing it in her pocket. On second thought she grabbed another. Being doubly sure wouldn't be a bad idea.

She succeeded in making it to a private bathroom in the back of Labor and Delivery without being seen. Briefly she'd considered going to Lucius's office bathroom—but what if he came in and started asking questions? She wasn't exactly known for her poker face.

Her hand shook as she removed the cellophane wrapper. She had to do this correctly. A false result would be more than she could stand.

She reviewed the directions as if she'd never read them before, then took the collection cup and caught her urine. Moments later she took an eyedropper and placed some of it in the required slot. Gradually a line appeared.

Her heart dropped in sadness as a negative sign showed, but seconds later it turned into a positive.

She was having a baby!

It would have been a lie if she'd said she wasn't elated.

A baby. Lucius's baby.

How would he feel about it? Would he be as happy as she was?

This baby would completely complicate her life.

Yes, but what joy it would bring.

She would have the precious baby she'd always dreamed of. Would he or she have beautiful blue eyes like its father?

Not wanting to shake Lucius's world from the bottom up without being absolutely sure, she took the other test. She smiled. Positive again.

Now the question was how she would tell Lucius...

She suspected he wouldn't be thrilled. But she was certain he would come around. Be as happy as her about it.

Amanda met him that evening at his car, as usual. At first their conversation revolved around the interesting patients they'd seen that day. But what she really wanted to do was shout out that she was pregnant. Still, she had to do it at the right time. While they were driving in traffic wasn't it.

A couple of times Lucius had to repeat what he'd said because she hadn't been listening. Her mind was rapidly moving through scenarios of how to tell him. She finally came to the conclusion that she'd have to treat it like a plastic bandage and just rip it off. Not hesitate further.

But the right time didn't come.

They prepared dinner together. She liked this time in their day the best. Lucius would keep her company in the kitchen. He seemed content. She had the idea he hadn't always been that way.

Still she couldn't say anything.

After dinner Lucius suggested a walk around the neighborhood. They held hands as they strolled. For a man who had not done it before she'd come to stay with him, he acted now as if he enjoyed greeting his neighbors. Amanda took a moment to dream of pushing a baby stroller along as they went.

They were getting ready for bed when Lucius came out of the bathroom and found her staring off into space.

"Is something wrong? Did something happen I need to know about?" he asked.

Concern laced his voice as he approached her.

Her hand covered her middle and she took a deep breath. "I'm pregnant."

CHAPTER NINE

"How did *that* happen?" Lucius glared at her.

The question would have been laughable if it hadn't been for the seriousness of the circumstances. He was a doctor who specialized in pregnancy. They were two adult professionals who should have been more careful.

"I think you're smart enough to figure that out," said Amanda.

"This isn't the time for your attempts at humor," he snapped.

He paced across the room.

"Of course I know *how* it happened. *When* is more like the right question."

Amanda gave him a pointed look. "That answer would be any day for the last three weeks and more often than not more than once. Take your pick."

Lucius had the good grace to look abashed. "Okay. Let's forget how and when and work on what we're going to do."

"That's not hard. I'm going to have it. Raise him or her and love him or her."

Lucius sounded much more unhappy about the baby than she'd anticipated.

"Amanda, I'm not father material. I certainly had no real example growing up. I'm not good husband material either. As a parent... I just don't think I'm what a child needs."

Her stomach turned sick and it had nothing to do with the baby.

Did he not recognize that all any child needed was love? She'd seen him with the babies at the clinic. He had what it took if he'd just trust himself.

"If that's how you feel then I'll do it by myself."

Lucius ran both hands through his hair. "Of course I'll provide for you both."

How like Lucius to think of practical considerations when all she and the baby needed was the intangible—his love.

"I don't want your money." Her words held bite.

He huffed. "What are we going to do...?"

Gone was the self-assured professional who seemed always to know his next move. They were talking in a circle now. As far as she was concerned there was no "we".

"*We're* not going to do anything. *I'm* going home on Saturday and I'll have a baby eight months later."

Lucius's face paled. He walked across the room and back.

They could have been so good together.

But once again they were on different sides of an issue. One that involved their lives. Their baby. Their future.

Lucius stopped pacing as her phone rang. It didn't do that often.

"I'm sorry, but I've got to get this," she told him. Into the phone, she said, "Hello? Yes, this is Amanda. I'll be there in fifteen minutes."

She hung up and stood. Her stomach took that moment to waver and crash. Grabbing the edge of the bed, she steadied herself.

Lucius hurried to her, fear in his eyes. "Are you okay?"

She raised her hand. "I'm fine. I just stood up too quickly, that's all. I've got to go to the clinic. Dr. Johannsson has tonight off and is out of town. Dr. Theodore was supposed to be on call but he has been in a car accident and doesn't know how long he'll be. Dr. Maxwell is on his way in, but he was at his beach house. A woman who's expecting triplets has chosen now to start having some trouble. I've got to go oversee things until a doctor can get there. I may need you to scrub in too."

Soon they were in the car on their way to the clinic. Lucius's hands gripped the steering wheel as he drove as fast as he safely could. He glanced at Amanda. She was speaking into her phone as she held a hand over her middle. Already her instincts were to protect their baby.

He knew he hadn't handled the last thirty minutes as well as he should have. But he couldn't believe he would soon be a father. *A father.* He glanced at Amanda. She'd be a good mother. She was all that was fine and decent in the world. She'd certainly made a difference in *his* life.

Now that the idea had had time to sink in he felt pride fill him. But despite that he still had no confidence he could be what Amanda and the baby needed for the long haul.

He had zero parenting skills. They had never been demonstrated on him. His father had had his work and his mother her books. He and Kirri had just been in the way. To think he might be husband material was laughable. He'd already proved he wasn't good at that. But what he *could* do was make sure they were financially cared for, regardless of whether or not Amanda wanted him to.

Less than half an hour later they were hurrying into Labor and Delivery. They headed straight to the locker room, where they changed into scrubs.

Amanda had spent the entire drive on her phone, talking to the nurses already in the labor area. From her tone of voice, the case sounded worse than expected.

As they scrubbed in Amanda said, "Dr. Maxwell is still a good thirty minutes out. The patient is showing signs of pre-eclampsia. One of the babies is already in distress. You're going to have to do a C-section. That baby isn't going to make it if you don't. May not even then. The patient is on her way to the OR now."

She pushed through the swinging door, using her hip.

"I'll see you in there."

She didn't wait for him to respond.

When he arrived in the OR some of the nurses were draping the woman for surgery. Machines blinked and the constant swish of three heart monitors filled the air.

Amanda was busy doing an examination with a vaginal stethoscope. Judging by the thin-lipped look of concentration on her face, the situation had turned dire.

He nodded to the woman's husband, who stood beside his wife, gripping her hand. Fear shadowed his face.

"Sir, I'm sorry, but you'll need to step out of the room now. When the babies are here and your wife is stable we'll let you return," Lucius said.

The man looked relieved to escape. A nurse led him out and returned.

Amanda finished her exam and he picked up a scalpel. "I'll do the section and then see to the patient. The babies are all yours."

She nodded. "I'll be ready. I want the one that's struggling first."

Lucius went to work. In less than five minutes Amanda handed off a tiny blue newborn to one of the other nurses in the room. He lifted the next one out and passed it to Amanda. She gave it to another waiting nurse. The last one was difficult. He had to do some maneuvering to get the baby out. Done, he handed the third one off.

A machine sounded the alarm.

"BP going down," his surgical nurse announced.

"Amanda, I'm going to need you over here."

He had to stop the bleeding or the mother would die.

Almost immediately Amanda stood beside him.

"Remove the placenta. I'll start massaging."

He had to do what the uterus was failing to do. With any luck uterine atony would soon kick in.

Amanda did as he said, then started pushing on the mother's abdomen.

"Blood pressure rising," the nurse declared.

The bleeding had slowed, but not stopped. He couldn't stop yet.

"Keep going. We've got to get this hemorrhaging completely under control. Get two units of whole blood started, STAT."

Amanda took the blood from the nurse who'd brought it to the table. With speed and efficiency she soon had it locked into the IV and running into the patient. She came to stand beside him and began mopping up the blood in the cavity.

Not soon enough for him, the nurse stated, "BP stable. Vitals stable."

He relaxed his shoulders.

"If you have this under control now I'll go speak to the father. I'm sure he needs a Valium by now."

Amanda moved toward the door and started pulling off her gloves.

Lucius had no doubt that if he were in the man's place he'd need one too. If he was with Amanda when their baby was born he was sure he'd feel the same way.

His chest constricted. He wouldn't be there. She'd be half a world away. He could only hope someone as dedicated as she was would be there to help her.

He finished stitching up the mother, refusing to let his mind wander further. If he did, he feared he might never be able to look at himself in the mirror again.

Half an hour later he handed off the care of the mother to Dr. Maxwell, who had finally arrived. Then Lucius went in search of Amanda.

He found her in the nursery, holding one of the babies he'd just delivered. There was an angelic expression on her face as she looked at the child. He was sure that look and many more like it would be on her face when their own baby arrived. But he wouldn't see any of them.

Fortifying himself, he stood in the doorway. "Amanda, are you ready to go home?"

His heart gasped with pain when she didn't look at him.

"I'll meet you at the car," she said.

"Okay."

He walked away, conscious of the fact that they

still had a difficult conversation ahead of them. But he hadn't changed his mind and he suspected Amanda hadn't either.

It had been a long time since Amanda had felt so tired. This pregnancy was already zapping her energy. To compound it, it had been an emotional discussion with Lucius and a difficult delivery afterward. She was done in. All she wanted was a hot shower and bed.

As she walked down the front hall of Lucius's home she made a left turn into the guest suite. Things weren't settled enough between them for her to think he'd want her in his bed.

"Goodnight. I'll see you tomorrow. Feel free to go into the clinic without me. I'll call a taxi."

Lucius made no response. She'd have been surprised if she was awake enough to hear it even if he had.

The next morning she woke to sunshine. It was late in the morning. She gazed out the window at the harbor, already teeming with activity. She would miss it. But not as much as she would Lucius.

She sighed. For the next four days she would focus on making good memories. Her hand went to her middle. She had something to look forward to with or without Lucius.

Moisture filled her eyes but she blinked it away. Was he still here at home? She wasn't ready to face him. If she did she might fall apart and beg him—for what? To stay? For them to find a way to make it work? For him to love her?

The house remained quiet. Undoubtedly Lucius had already left. She needed to go to work as well.

She looked at the bedside table to see crackers and a glass of soda waiting. A sad smile came to her lips. Even though things weren't good between them Lucius was still concerned about her.

On her way to the bathroom she noticed the head indentation on the other pillow. Had Lucius slept there too last night?

Unsure what to make of that, she knew her heart couldn't help but feel encouraged.

An hour later, at the clinic, she knocked on Lucius's office door since his assistant was not behind her desk. Amanda wasn't confident of her welcome, but they needed to talk—even if it was just about living arrangements.

"Come in."

Lucius looked up in surprise when she entered. He stood, but stayed behind his desk. Uncertainty the size of an iceberg loomed between them. She hated that. Had it only been last week that he'd sent her over the moon with just the touch of his hands in this very room?

How quickly life changed.

"I just wanted to let you know I've made arrangements to move back to the hotel this evening."

He looked stricken, and then panicked, as if he had never considered the possibility of her moving out. His fingers gripped the front edge of his desk.

"I wish you wouldn't do that," he said. "You'll only be here a few more nights and I think we can survive those under the same roof together." He came around the desk, his hand outstretched. "Amanda, I want us to remain friends. After all we'll have a child together."

"I want us to be friends as well, but I don't want to make you uncomfortable in your own home."

She didn't want to go. Truth be known, she'd like to stay with him forever.

"You won't. I'd like you to stay. Please."

Once again she found herself agreeing to something she wasn't completely sure about. "All right. Thank you."

He opened his mouth and then closed it, as if he wanted to say more but wasn't sure how to begin. The self-assured doctor wasn't acting that way today.

A few moments later he asked, "Could we talk tonight?"

"Sure."

Her heart fell. She wouldn't be looking forward to that discussion. They could chat about anything he wanted, but her mind was already made up about the baby and what she would accept from him.

Nothing less than his love.

For her, a baby shouldn't be a way to receive love, but a product of love.

That evening, after dinner, Lucius found himself standing over Amanda like a thundercloud ready to pour rain. That hadn't been his intention. He'd wanted them to find a compromise that they could live with—really one that *he* could live with. And so far Amanda had shot down all his suggestions.

Right now, she was watching him calmly from the sofa. She wasn't going to change her mind about her plans. At this rate all he would have when she left was a path worn in his hardwood floor from the number of times he'd walked back and forth in frustration.

The stubborn woman hadn't moved an inch. She wanted something he was incapable of giving.

After another trip across the room he flopped down to the sofa cushions. He could hear his father saying, *"Pull yourself together, son. West men don't act like that."* Lucius stood up again. He would give it one more shot.

"Stay here. You like it here. I'll share my view with you for as long as you want. We'll make a spot at the clinic for you."

Her gaze remained fixed on him. "Is that all you're offering?"

"I don't know what you mean..."

"I'm not surprised." She shook her head. Her mouth formed a sad smile. "It's not going to work between us. You're sorry about the baby and you feel responsible. I didn't plan this but I'm happy about it."

He glared at her. Here he was, twisting in the wind. In an odd way he suspected his world was coming apart, but he didn't understand how to stop it imploding. He needed to get control back. Amanda sat there coolly telling him that she'd be having his baby thousands of miles away from him and he just had to deal with it.

"Don't worry, Lucius. We'll both be fine."

He forced himself to sit down again, his fingers biting into the sofa cushions. *Without him?* She couldn't have hurt him more if she'd physically punched him.

"I'll let you know when it's born."

"Will that be by mail, email or text?" he spat.

Amanda flinched and turned away from him. Her voice sounded flat when she said, "I'll call the minute I can. I'd never keep you from knowing about your child. If I'd wanted to do that I wouldn't have told you in the first place."

Something gripped his heart and squeezed, making his chest physically hurt. He might believe he wasn't husband material, and he suspected he wouldn't be any better as a father, but he wanted to know his child. He cared. More than she knew. More than he wanted to show.

He waited until she looked at him. "You can't keep my child from me. He or she *will* know its father."

"I would never do that." Her words sounded sincere but still her eyes remained anxious.

Lucius ran his hand through his hair. "I know. I'm just not thinking right these days."

She turned toward him and reached out a hand, but didn't touch him. "How much you see your child will be totally up to you."

"I wish you would reconsider staying here." He wouldn't continue to beg.

She gave him a pleading look. "I don't want to argue with you, but you can't control everything."

Lucius jumped to his feet. "I'm not *trying* to control everything!"

"Right. You control the clinic. Your work. You tried to control Kirri but she broke away—and she had to go all the way to Atlanta to do it. You even try to control your emotions. You're running scared, out of control, and you can't stand it."

He jerked as if she had actually hit him.

Continuing as if she'd been banking the words for a while now, and had finally opened the vault door, she said, "Your childhood with your father has affected how you see the world, and it isn't always correct. Still, it's understandable. You've had a failed marriage when you were raised to believe that failure wasn't an option. Yet sometimes things happen in life that we don't always plan."

She placed her hand over her stomach.

"Sometimes we just don't make the right choices and it ends badly. That's called life. Some things are out of our control. That doesn't mean we shouldn't try again. Or that we should consider ourselves failures."

Lucius glared down at her, his hands on his hips. "What are you saying? Are you saying you think we ought to get married? If that will keep you from leaving, then that's what we'll do."

She stood, went to the window and looked out blankly, her shoulders slumped. "That's a proposal that any woman would be *dying* to hear. Thanks, Lucius, but *no,* thanks."

"I'm sorry—I did that all wrong." He started to go to her but then held himself in check.

Amanda shook her head, still not looking at him. "I don't think you know what you want clearly enough that you should be involving me or this baby."

That hurt—especially coming from her. It sounded too final.

He couldn't help but fight back. "Don't start psychoanalyzing me."

She turned to face him. "I'm not. I'm just stating how I see it. I've made a decision to go home at the end of the week. I'll let you know when the baby is born. You're welcome to see the baby whenever you choose. That is totally up to you. I want this child. I can support it. You need to figure out how involved you want to be and then cut yourself some slack. It might come as a surprise to you to realize that you *are* father material. That's something I already know."

"How do you know that?" He watched her closely.

"I've told you this before. I've seen you with the babies. Tough guy that you are, you go to the nursery to hold the babies when you need some downtime. Guess what? Your secret is out. You're an old softy."

She said it with complete confidence. Stated it as fact. He couldn't have done the same.

"But that doesn't mean anything."

"It's a darn good start. We didn't intend to make a baby. It happened. I won't call it a mistake. I love this baby already. That's why I can't stay here and be your mistress, or have you provide me with a job or a roof over my head. I have pride too, Lucius."

"If you ask me, you have too much," he murmured.

He could have kicked himself. The moment he made the statement he knew he'd said the wrong thing. But now he had to back it up. If not to get it off his chest then for her own good.

"You've become too accustomed to being self-sufficient. You can't see that maybe you could use my help. You think men are either incapable of being what you need or that they will disappoint you, so you never let them get close enough to prove you wrong."

She turned to face him. "That's not—"

"You think we're all your stepfather. Wanting a pretty picture that doesn't include you. You push us all away because you think we're going to leave you anyway."

"I do not!"

"Sure you do. You're doing it right now. I'm not measuring up to the mark you've set so you're leaving. Not even considering other options. At least stay a little while longer and let's see if we can figure out a better way than you and the baby being thousands of miles away from me. Have a little trust in me. In *us*."

"Would you want me to stay if it weren't for the baby? Part of our relationship was built on the fact it would be short-lived. I was part of a package deal when my mother married my stepfather. It didn't work out well for me. It won't be that way again—not for me or my child. You only want me to stay because of the baby. That's not a good enough reason for me."

"So we're back to me marrying you, are we?"

"I've never even mentioned marriage! You're the one that keeps bringing it up. But, while we're on the subject, you and I both know it would have never have come up as an option if I hadn't gotten pregnant."

With her head held high she started toward the guest suite.

"I think I've had enough talking for one day. Goodnight."

Lucius stood speechless. He wanted to follow her, but now wasn't the time.

He had a lot of thinking to do. A long hard swim was what he needed…

Amanda lay in the dark bedroom with the door open, listening to the water splash as Lucius swam lap after lap in the pool. It sounded as if he were swimming for his life.

Why couldn't he understand that she had been trying to tell him something important? That she wanted his love. Not the job, the view, or to live in Sydney, but him. For a man who prided himself on his intelligence, he'd missed the point where she was concerned.

Sometime later the door to the hall opened and then softly closed. Seconds later the mattress dipped and Lucius gathered her into his arms. Her body had become used to having him close, longed for him.

Hadn't he told her weeks ago that under his roof they would share the same bed regardless of any disagreement between them? It wasn't a good idea, but she couldn't send him away.

"Lucius," she said, so softly it was a whisper.

"Shh… Go to sleep."

He brought her close and she rested her head on his shoulder. She waited, anticipating he'd make love to her, but he made no move to do so. He'd placed another row of bricks on the wall he had started building between them.

With a deep, dejected exhalation she closed her eyes, but didn't find sleep for a long time.

Lucius was gone when she woke the next morning. A plate of crackers and a glass of bubbly soda sat on the bedside table.

A while later Amanda got dressed for work and joined him in the kitchen.

Lucius sat drinking his coffee and staring off into space. He looked as miserable as she felt. His hair was tousled, as if he'd been running his fingers through it. Her fingers itched to touch it, to smooth it into place, but she wasn't sure he would allow it.

She would miss Lucius so badly.

She'd feared some of the antagonism from their discussion the night before might bleed over into the morning but it seemed that by mutual tacit agreement they'd decided that being civil over the next few days would be the answer. No tension filled the room, but instead something much worse hovered over them: the melancholy mist of hopelessness.

"Thank you for the crackers. They do make a difference." She gave him a weak smile.

"You're welcome. I hate that you don't feel well."

His eyes had lost their shine. *She* hated that.

Taking a bite of her toast, she said, "It's just part of the process."

"I sort of feel guilty."

There was that soft heart of his she loved so much.

A genuine smile came to her lips. "Don't. If it's any help, I think morning sickness is well worth the outcome. I'll meet you at the car in a few minutes."

The rest of their days together went much the same way. They lived as roommates, with that brick wall between them growing ever higher. Except at night, when it turned into glass and Lucius came to her bed.

Yet the wall still remained.

More than once she questioned if she was doing the right thing by leaving. Why couldn't she stay? After all, he'd offered her everything she'd ever dreamed of—everything but his love. And in time maybe that would come.

Lucius was a good man. He would be there for her and their child. Couldn't that be enough for her?

But what if she stayed and in time he decided he didn't want her? Other men had. What if Lucius decided she was too opinionated, too driven, too demanding? She still wanted a successful career, and she was still that person who stood up to him, questioned him. Could Lucius accept that?

Worse, what if he decided he no longer wanted her and started seeing another woman? Could she stand being close enough to see that happen?

By then their child might have gotten to know Lucius well, and she wouldn't be able to return to America without ripping her child away from its father, causing untold misery for everyone.

The what-ifs continued to whirl around in her mind. The only answer that came back as a sure thing was that Lucius hadn't said anything about loving her. If they'd loved each other she knew they would be able to work anything out. Without love between them she didn't see any hope for them.

They didn't discuss the future, even though she remained hyper-aware that she would be leaving soon. The breach between them widened, as if he were already slowly breaking away from her. How big would it become when she returned to America?

By Friday she felt sick—and it had nothing to do with being pregnant. Tomorrow morning she would get on a plane and fly out of Lucius's city—out of his life and out of his arms.

Only with a fortitude she hadn't known she possessed did Amanda keep moving forward at work, smiling at all the right times and saying all the right things.

That evening the clinic staff had a going-away party for her. It just punctuated the fact that her time with Lucius had come to an end. She glanced at him. He didn't look like he was in a partying mood either. In fact, he appeared as if he would rather be anywhere but there. He'd spent most of the last hour leaning against a wall with a drink in his hand, glaring at her.

All the clinic staff came to speak to her, and many of them she hugged. To a few she promised to stay in touch. She knew she wouldn't. If she was going to survive she'd have to make a clean cut of it or she'd never get over Lucius. She would never do that anyway.

When one of the men hugged her she noticed that Lucius moved away from the wall and stood ramrod-straight. For a second she feared he might even grab the guy and yank him away from her. She broke the embrace and turned to another person waiting to talk to her.

After the party, Lucius helped her carry her going-away presents to the car.

"You've really made an impression on my clinic staff. I won't be the only one to miss you."

"Lucius, please don't. It's hard enough as it is…"

They drove home with a silence filling the car as deep as the ocean that would soon be between them. They went their separate ways in the front hallway without a word.

She finished packing, then ate a simple meal while watching through the kitchen window as Lucius swam. Finished with her meal, she showered and went to bed. There, she lay tense and wide awake. Would he come to her tonight?

Her heart pounded as the door opened. Moments later Lucius put his arms around her. Amanda turned and ran her fingers over his chest. She couldn't believe she was going to bare her soul, but she couldn't leave without telling him what she wanted.

"Lucius, I need you to love me."

That was all the invitation he seemed to need before his mouth found hers. But she was looking for love from his heart, not just from his body. He still didn't understand—or didn't want to.

The next morning Lucius drove her to the airport. They said nothing on the ride there. Everything had been said already.

She insisted he drop her off at the curb. He took her suitcase out of the trunk and placed it beside her. Their gazes met. Could he see the pain and disappointment in hers? Her chest constricted, as if the world was pressing down on her. She fought for air.

Surely these feelings would pass with time?

A great deal of it, she feared.

"Goodbye, Amanda. I'll be expecting your call."

Lucius's voice held no emotion at all. That brick wall had gone way too high. They had become strangers.

"Bye, Lucius. I've enjoyed my visit Down Under and I wish you a happy life."

She walked off as her heart exploded into a thousand pain-filled pieces.

CHAPTER TEN

WITH A FORCE of will that Amanda hadn't known she possessed, she took the handle of her suitcase and started toward the airport doors. Every fiber of her being wanted to turn and run back into Lucius's open arms. The problem was that his arms wouldn't be open. He didn't want her for forever and she wouldn't settle for less. She and the baby deserved love, not obligation.

Lucius cared for her, and even for this baby too, but he feared he wouldn't be enough for them. She didn't care if he wasn't perfect. She just needed his love. He couldn't bring himself to say it, but she believed he did love her in his own way. He just didn't recognize it, and she couldn't stay on the chance that he might one day comprehend it. If he hadn't figured it out over the last few days there was a real chance he never would.

When she got to the airline desk she learned she'd been upgraded to First Class. She would have a seat that turned into a bed for her return flight. She had no doubt that Lucius was responsible for making those arrangements. He continued to take care of her.

She held her tears in check until she found her seat on the plane. There she let them go.

She'd found a real home and friends in Sydney. It tore her heart out to leave. Even the staff at the clinic had begged her to stay, or at least come back for a visit. She'd promised to come if she had a chance. She couldn't guarantee that would happen. Returning to Lucius's clinic would be too painful.

His outlook on life had been shaped by his parents and by his broken marriage. He'd thrown himself into his work. Facts and figures were always right or wrong, black or white, and they required no sentiment. He'd even treated his sister as more of a test experiment than a sibling relationship. Emotionally, he was as inexperienced as the newborn babies she helped to deliver.

And she couldn't accept what Lucius had offered because of her own background. Settling for what looked like love? She wasn't willing to do that. The pain of leaving him would never be as great as staying and knowing he didn't love her the way she loved him. She wasn't willing to live every day hoping she would hear those three special words and never have them uttered.

More than one person on the plane was giving her a concerned look. The steward asked if she was all right. Pushing a tear away from her cheek, she assured him that she was.

Exhausted and emotionally drained, she went to sleep. When she woke there was a cup of soda and some crackers next to her. Her eyes watered again. Lucius must have left special instructions.

When the steward came by again he said, "Congratulations on the baby."

"How did you know?"

He grinned and nodded toward the crackers. "The breakfast of a mother-to-be."

The one shining diamond in this entire mess between her and Lucius was the baby. It was time she focused on it and not on what couldn't be. Wallowing in negatives wasn't what she needed to do. What she should be grateful for was the precious life inside her.

She landed in Atlanta and took a taxi to her apartment. It seemed like she'd been gone for years instead of only a few weeks. In an odd way, despite all her personal items, it was like she'd left her home thousands of miles away below the equator.

Sitting on her couch, she pulled a pillow to her chest and let the tears go again. She'd had to leave the pillows she'd bought in Sydney behind, because they hadn't fitted in her luggage. They were still on her bed at Lucius's house. Would he throw them out now that she was gone?

The diamond bracelet she had intended to leave behind, but in the end she hadn't been able to bring herself to do so. It was safely tucked in her purse. When the baby grew up, if it was a daughter, she would give it to her—or, if it was a son, to him, for his wife.

She had to get a grip. There was mail to go

through, food to buy, her suitcase to unpack and she needed to call her family. Sitting around floundering in her own pain wasn't going to get her anywhere.

Monday morning, she stepped off the elevator on the fifth floor of the Medical Innovations Center and entered the Piedmont Women and Baby Pavilion. She went stock-still when the first person she saw was Kirri West—now Sawyer.

Amanda hadn't thought it through that she would still be working with Lucius's sister. It was difficult enough that they favored each other physically, but what if Kirri talked about him or he came for a visit?

Amanda's stomach swirled and she gripped the counter and closed her eyes.

"Hey, come sit down..."

It was Kirri's voice. Amanda knew that accent. Heard a deeper one like it in her dreams each night.

Kirri gripped her arm and led her to an exam room. "You okay? I don't usually have people going weak in the knees when they see me." Kirri grinned.

A gorgeous woman, Amanda was sure that Kirri received plenty of wolf whistles when her husband, Dr. Ty Sawyer wasn't around to fend them off.

"You aren't the problem. A combination of jet-lag, too little breakfast, the humidity and the Atlanta traffic are more like it."

Amanda moved to sit up. Her stomach chose that moment to revolt.

"Pan."

Kirri quickly handed her a kidney-shaped plastic pan. When Amanda was more herself Kirri asked, "Did you bring one of our bugs home from Australia?"

Amanda had brought something home, but it wasn't an illness. Still, she wasn't prepared to tell Kirri she was pregnant by her brother. That seemed like something that Lucius should share with his sister.

"I'm fine. Give me a few minutes and I'll get it together. I guess I was afraid no one would notice I'd been gone so I had to make a scene."

"We noticed you were gone. I hear we're lucky to get you back because they wanted to keep you in Sydney. I want to hear all about your trip, what you learned, and if my brother is still whispering babies into existence. How about lunch one day soon?"

"Sure. That sounds great." Amanda hoped it wouldn't be soon.

Kirri's phone rang. She answered and told the person on the other end she would be there in a minute. "I've got to go. You get something to eat—and go slow today, until you get your system back on Georgia time."

"Will do."

With relief Amanda watched Kirri leave, then took a few minutes to gather herself and start her day again.

After that unimpressive first day back at work she got up the next morning early enough to eat and drink something. Lucius had always seen to it, but now it was her responsibility.

Amanda managed to avoid Kirri. She just wasn't ready to talk about her time in Australia—especially with Lucius's sister. When other people asked her how her trip had been she gave them a brief description of the clinic, stating that it was brilliant and innovative and that Sydney was beautiful.

It wasn't until one day when she had been assigned an early-morning delivery that she saw Kirri again, other than brief passes in the hall. Kirri had been asked to consult on the case.

As bad luck would have it, Amanda's stomach chose then to flip. Running late, she'd not had a chance to eat before coming into work that morning.

"I'm sorry," she said to the room in general, and ran for the door.

A few minutes later Kirri came into the staff locker room, where Amanda sat on the bench after coming out of the bathroom. Amanda wanted to groan.

"I'm starting to think either I make you sick or we need to run some tests."

Amanda looked at her and shook her head. "There's no need. I know what's wrong."

Kirri's eyes held compassion. "Would you like to tell me?"

That would be a resounding *no*—but Amanda wasn't going to take out her disappointment in Lucius on his sister.

"I'm pregnant."

Kirri continued to watch her. "I'm guessing this happened while you were in Sydney. Is it anybody I know?"

Amanda groaned out loud this time. "Yeah, rather well. It's your brother."

Kirri squealed and clapped her hands. "I'm going to be an auntie! Lucius did tell me over the phone that he thought you were an exceptional nurse, and bright. That's about as high praise as Lucius is capable of. But I had no idea you were seeing each other. He knows about the baby?"

"He does. I found out a few days before I left. I told him." Amanda looked at the floor.

Kirri gasped. Her voice held disbelief when she asked, "And he let you go?"

"He didn't want to. But he didn't make the right offer for me to stay."

"I see."

And somehow Amanda thought she did.

"Why am I not surprised?" Kirri shook her head.

"I'd like to keep this between us, if that's okay," said Amanda. "I'm not ready to tell the entire clinic yet. I'm still trying to adjust to the idea myself."

Kirri nodded. "I understand."

"I'd also prefer that you don't discuss it with Lucius. He's made his decision and I've made mine."

And she wasn't happy about either one.

Kirri placed her arm on Amanda's shoulder. "You love him, don't you?"

Amanda met eyes so like Lucius's. "Very much."

Neither of them said anything for a few minutes.

"I'll honor your wishes for as long as I can. After all, this is my niece or nephew too. I may have to say something—especially if the parents are too hardheaded to get their acts together."

Kirri gave Amanda's shoulders a squeeze.

"When Lucius loves it's deeply and completely. He'll protect those he loves to his dying breath. The problem is he has a difficult time expressing that love outside of actions."

Kirri paused just long enough for Amanda to look at her.

"Sometimes even *I* have to meet him more than halfway. Think about that."

That weekend Amanda met her mother at a café in Virginia Highlands. It was one of Amanda's favorite neighborhoods. In a way, it reminded her of Lucius's neighborhood. The homes were older here, and had been refurbished. There was a warmness and friendliness about the area that relaxed her. She needed that today.

Her mother was already waiting at a table when Amanda arrived. She rose and gave Amanda a tight hug and kiss. "It's so good to see you, honey. It has been too long. How was your trip to Australia?"

That was all that it took to bring tears to her eyes.

Her mother reached across the table and took her hand. "Tell me."

Amanda did. Every detail. And felt better for it.

Her mother smiled. "So I'm going to be a grandmother."

Amanda's hand automatically went to her middle, which it often did these days. "That seems to be the case."

They had finished their meal when Amanda said, "Can I ask you something?"

The waitress refilled their glasses and left.

"Of course, honey."

Amanda didn't want to make things uncomfortable between them, but she had to know. Therefore she had to ask. She should've done it long ago.

"Why has my stepfather never loved me?"

Her mother hissed and her face looked stricken, then unbearably sad. "I'm so sorry you've felt that way. I guess some of it has been my fault."

How could it have been her mother's doing? She'd never been anything but loving.

"He does love you, but he has a poor way of showing it. I know you saw him as differentiating between how he felt about you and your brother and sister, but it wasn't as wide a gap as you believe. At one time, when you were little, you would climb in his lap and you were very close—and then, as if a light had been turned off, you refused to have anything to do with him. From then on the distance between you just grew. He tried really hard for a time to reconcile with you. I encouraged him, but didn't push, and the rift just got wider."

"I heard you arguing over my prom dress. He didn't want to buy it." Amanda fiddled with her napkin corner then looked at her mother.

Her lips had formed a thin line. "He wanted you to have a more expensive dress and I said we couldn't afford it."

Amanda was heartsick. "Is that really true?"

"Of course it is."

"Mom, you should have sat me down and straightened me out. Not let me act that way toward him."

"Honey, I don't think it was as bad as you think

it was. Some of it we put down to you being a kid, and then a normal hormonal teenager. You were always such a determined girl. It was hard to change your mind once you got a thought in your head. We just had to wait it out until you figured it out differently."

"Like right now?"

Had she been the same way with Lucius? Had she made up her mind and disregarded everything he'd said and felt about the situation?

Her mother gave her a wry smile and shrugged.

Amanda couldn't have been more mortified and disappointed in herself. She'd been so unfair to her stepfather and it appeared she had been doing it most of her life.

"Do you think he'll accept my apology after so many years?"

"Honey, I know he will. It's never too late to tell someone you're sorry and that you care about them."

Later that evening as Amanda tossed and turned, begging for sleep, the memory of Lucius's face when she'd left him at the airport kept running through her mind.

Her heart squeezed. He'd been hurting. A man who never seemed lost for words had said nothing. He knew his own mind—of that she had no doubt—but she wasn't sure he knew his own heart. Even then she'd wanted to reach out and soothe that look off his face.

Amanda rolled over and pulled a pillow to her, wishing it was Lucius. She missed his warmth and the gentle heaviness of his arm which had always been around her. The one that made her feel wanted, as if she belonged.

A sob escaped her.

Tired of crying herself to sleep, she revisited her mother's words. She'd been completely wrong about her stepfather. How had she spent so many years being so mistaken? Why hadn't she seen what was around her? She and her stepfather had both suffered for so long unnecessarily. Worse, she'd let their relationship color all the others she'd had—especially the one with Lucius.

How he must hate her. She'd left pregnant with his child, promising him nothing but a phone call after it was born. What kind of person was she to leave the man she loved that way? She should have done better than that. Given him a few more weeks to think about how he felt. But she hadn't done that, had she? She'd made up her mind and that was that.

Would Lucius accept her apology? Could he possibly feel the same way about her as she did him? Was he just afraid to say it?

She been so dogmatic about returning to America she hadn't given him a chance. She'd chosen her reality instead of seeing it for what it was.

Based on what Kirri said, Lucius showed his love in actions rather than words. Through those she had no doubt she'd been cherished by Lucius. She knew what it was like to live under his protection. Even when he'd tried to check out emotionally he'd still come to her bed each night. He'd only held her until she'd asked for more. Even on the day she'd left he'd placed soda and crackers beside her bed in the morning.

Lucius had offered her everything, but had stopped short of saying he loved her. Was Kirri right? Was it just too difficult for him to do? Had Amanda pushed him away like she'd done her stepfather?

Maybe Lucius had been right when he had accused her of being so afraid of abandonment she'd never opened herself up enough to give a man a true chance.

That would stop now. She planned to go after what she wanted—Lucius, a father for her child, and a chance at happiness.

Lucius left the airport confident that letting Amanda go was the right thing to do. He wasn't the man she needed to build her life around. Or the man who should be the father to their child. He could never give her all that she needed or deserved. His time, affections and support would always be dictated by outside forces.

That was who he was and how he lived his life. If he tried to make a stronger commitment he knew it would end in disaster. He cared too much for Amanda and the baby to have them depend on him and him let them down. He had to accept that Amanda and his baby were lost to him forever.

Returning to his house, he didn't make it any further than Amanda's bedroom door. Disgusted with himself, he looked at the bed. Each night he'd gone to her like a junkie, looking for his next fix, unable to stay away. They had made love for the last time with such tenderness and now the bed mocked him. It was made up and neat, like their relationship should have been, and yet it hadn't happened that way. Instead what had been between them had become messy, storm-blown and painful.

In the center of the bedspread were Amanda's two pillows—the ones that she'd insisted she bring with her after she'd had to move out of the apartment. To him they represented the finality of their break. She'd left them behind like she'd left him behind.

Lucius turned and stalked down the hall, went out to his car and drove off. He drove and drove and drove. The destination didn't matter. What he desperately wanted to do was forget.

It had turned dark when he pulled into a small hotel on some highway and rented a room for the night.

He couldn't face his house again. And fear filled him that he might feel the same about the clinic. Even the city had changed for him.

Amanda, and memories of her, being with her, had colored his world. He just had to wait until the memories of her burned away like a morning fog and cleared his mind.

His greatest fear was that it might never happen.

Still, he had the weekend to recover. He'd have no choice but to move on come Monday. There was the clinic to run and his research to see about. As a gifted, mature adult he needed to get on with his life. Amanda had gone and he needed to accept that. Learn to live with it.

Late the next evening he returned to his house. It didn't have the same appeal to him as it once had. During the time Amanda had been there the house had become a home. He'd liked it that way. Wanted it back.

This time as he passed her bedroom he closed the door. Maybe if he didn't look at the bed every time he came and went it would be easier. He had no doubt he was making excuses. The door being closed wouldn't remove Amanda from his mind.

He went to his office and checked his messages with the hope that there would be one from her. There were none.

Thankfully the next week was so busy he even managed a few hours of not letting Amanda creep into his thoughts. He found that the only time she remained completely out of his mind was when he saw his patients. His lab work was suffering the most. Being in a room all alone just made matters worse. It gave him too much time to think, and the processes were too much by rote.

He finally gave up one day, totally disgusted. This had to stop.

His staff had started to give him odd looks. They would quit talking when he walked up. Or whisper when they didn't think he was around. More than one looked as if they were too scared to approach him.

His world was crumbling around him and he didn't know how to glue it back together.

In a strange way, he was frightening himself. He wasn't eating, he slept on a sofa or in one of the extra bedrooms—if he slept at all. He dreaded going to work and he hated being at home. He was in a black place and he saw no light.

The weekend loomed large and dark before him. Because of that he decided he might as well visit his father. He couldn't make it any worse.

Saturday morning Lucius drove the hour and a half to an exclusive nursing home on the north side of the city. He recognized that he was only going to see his father out of obligation and not devotion.

The man who had been such a demanding figure in Lucius's life had deteriorated in body but his mind remained sharp. When he entered his father's room the nurse sitting at his bedside stood and nodded, then left them alone. His father leaned against the headboard propped up by pillows with his eyes closed. The TV was turned down low, as if it were just background noise.

"Hello, Father."

The old man opened his eyes slowly. "Lucius."

"How have you been?" Lucius took a seat in the chair.

"About the same. I'm stuck in here."

Until that moment Lucius hadn't realized that anything in particular had brought him there today. "Did you love my mother?" he asked suddenly.

His father blinked. His watery old eyes met Lucius's gaze. "Not the way I should have."

"Why?"

"Because I didn't know how to be a good doctor and a husband and father at the same time. It's my greatest regret."

That statement was like a direct punch to Lucius's chest.

"I did great things as a doctor but I pushed my wife and family away in the process. By the time I realized that it was too late. Your mother was in her own world, you'd become a man too much like me, and Kirri…" He shook his head and sighed.

Lucius stared at his father. This conversation was the furthest from anything he'd ever expected to have with his father.

"Work doesn't keep you warm at night, or give

you a smile in the morning, or visit you when you become an old man," his father murmured, and then he drifted off to sleep again.

Lucius sat there contemplating what he'd just learned. The foundations of his life had just been shaken.

Had he followed too closely in his father's footsteps? Not only professionally but in his personal life as well? His father had failed in the family arena, certainly, and had made choices that Lucius didn't want to repeat.

Did he drive all the women in his life away like his father had? Lucius had done that with his first wife by not being there, and now he'd driven Amanda and his baby away as well. Did he want to one day find himself lying in a bed alone, wishing he had done better?

Was he really that self-obsessed? A man who couldn't see what he had before him?

What if another man came into Amanda's life? He would become her lover and the baby's father.

Lucius gripped the arm of the chair until his knuckles turned white. He couldn't stay on that train of thought. It hurt too much.

He had always believed part of his and his ex-wife's problems had been because she wasn't involved in his world. Apparently he'd been wrong. Even with Amanda, who understood his work, he had disagreed, but they had managed to get through it. Their relationship had mattered enough to her for them to fight, make up and move on.

Amanda had asked for his help when she delivered another woman's babies, but she wouldn't ask him for help with their own. What did that say about him? Had he really made her think she was that unwanted, or that he cared so little about her and the baby? What if she had trouble delivering, like the mother with the triplets, and he wasn't there? What if Amanda had a difficult pregnancy and he wasn't around to help? She was already having bad morning sickness.

It was his job to care for and protect her and their child. That was what a loving relationship should be about. Caring for each other. And she was thousands of miles away because he couldn't say he loved her.

Did he? He realized he did. Very much.

Had he been so focused on his own shortcomings that he'd been too afraid to express his love?

She'd asked him to love her in bed that last night. And he had, but not as she'd really wanted him to. She'd needed to hear him say the words. To know she was wanted, needed and precious to him. To be told that not just physically, but to hear it said out loud to the world.

Amanda was his chance at real love. A way to change his past. Make his life better. He understood that now. She'd been an outsider growing up. Had given part of herself to people all her professional life and they had all let her down. She wanted to be loved for who she was, not because she carried his baby. To be loved for herself.

And what had he offered her? A move to another country. Giving up the job she'd worked so hard for. Sleeping in his bed with no promises from him and giving up her pride. What kind of egotistical fool must he have sounded like?

He wanted to rebuild his life—with Amanda by his side.

Scooting back on the examination table, Amanda prepared for her first prenatal appointment. She fidgeted with excitement, and yet sadness surrounded her because Lucius wasn't there. If things had been different they would be sharing this moment.

She had no doubt he would be an attentive father and she intended to give him that chance. In two days she would fly back to Australia. She planned to take him up on his offer of a job.

He didn't deserve for her to take his child so far away from him. If Lucius still wanted her at his house and in his bed she would accept that too. She understood who he was. He'd showed her he cared through his actions. From all she'd seen, she had been well loved.

The obstetrician finished her exam. "I pronounce you fit to fly. And I understand you'll be getting the best care there is in Australia. We'll miss you here. Now, I have a few more lines on the chart to fill out and then you can get dressed."

There was some type of commotion going on in the hall. Amanda glanced at the door.

The door swung open just as the obstetrician asked, "Would you like to include the father's name on the chart?"

Lucius stalked in. "Yes, she would. Dr. Lucius West."

"Lucius!" The word came out on a cloud of shock and joy. Her heart fluttered. What was he doing there? Did she dare to hope he'd come after her?

He stepped to her side and took her hand. It wasn't what she'd expected him to do. She'd anticipated him going straight into doctor mode.

Instead he demanded of the other doctor, "How is she?"

With a slight smile on her face the obstetrician answered, "It's nice to finally meet you, Dr. West."

Lucius nodded, but his eyes never left Amanda. It was as if he were drinking her in. Somehow wanting to absorb her, adoring her. It was a rather wonderful feeling.

The obstetrician continued, "She's in perfect health. She's free to fly."

"You're sure?" Lucius sounded anxious. "Fly?" His face took on a look of confusion.

"Amanda, I'm done here. You may dress now."

The doctor smiled and left the room, leaving her and Lucius alone.

"What are you doing here?" She scooted to the end of the exam table, preparing to get down. She needed clothes on to handle this conversation.

Lucius offered her his hand. She took it and climbed from the table. Covering herself the best she could with the paper wrap, and without saying a word, she hurried behind the screen.

"Lucius, why are you here?" she asked again.

"I came for my heart."

He sounded as if he was standing just on the other side of the curtain. So close but still so far away.

Fear filled her. Was he sick?

"What's wrong with your heart?"

"You have it. I can't breathe or think or live or work without you."

Amanda's breath caught. Did he mean what she hoped he did?

"Are you dressed yet?" His voice was rough and still so close.

"Not completely."

The curtain was whipped back. "I like you better without clothes on anyway."

Lucius took her into his arms, pulling her to him and kissing her like he would never let her go. Amanda had found heaven. She ran her hands over his shoulders and cupped his face, frantically returning his kisses.

Finally he pulled his head back just enough so she could see his beautiful eyes.

"I love you, Amanda. I love you."

"And I love you, with all my heart."

A quick knock on the door made them look that way. Amanda pulled the paper sheet around her and stood behind Lucius as Kirri stepped in.

"I heard a buzz that there was a famous Australian doctor causing a scene down here. I had to come see who it might be. Imagine my surprise to learn it's just my brother."

She came over and gave him a tight hug and a kiss on the cheek.

"Hey, Amanda. I'm glad to see this blockhead finally came around. I was going to give him one more week, then I was going to break my promise and have a talk with him."

Amanda couldn't do anything but stand there, stunned.

"Tomorrow night you'll both be expected at my house for dinner. The family will be there."

Kirri made it sound like being with the Sawyer side of her family was like a recipe for happiness and she wanted to share it.

"See you then." She went out the door, singing, "I'm going to be an auntie… I'm going to be auntie…"

Lucius and Amanda laughed. It felt so good to do it again. All the laughter had been sucked out of her life since she'd left Lucius.

He kissed her again. "Finish getting your clothes on. We need to talk somewhere with some privacy."

Amanda pulled on her clothes as Lucius waited by the door, watching her. Her hands shook at his intense stare that flickered with desire. She'd missed him all the way to her soul.

Lucius did a fine job of driving to her apartment. To her mind he was exceptional at everything.

They walked hand in hand to the elevator. As the doors closed he took her into his arms and kissed her. It was a kiss of craving, and yet a new element had been added. An element of tenderness, a promise, and the gift of all of Lucius's heart. It was as if two cells in Lucius's lab that had been free-floating had found each other, forming a perfect match.

Inside her place, Lucius looked around. "I like your apartment. It's very you."

She huffed. "It has no view like yours."

"What it has is you. That makes all the difference." He took her hand and led her to the sofa. "We should talk."

She sat. He took a spot far enough away that he could face her while holding both of her hands. "Amanda, I've been an idiot. I'm sorry. When you left anything that was good, right and wonderful in my life went with you. I was even going to let my child be raised thousands of miles away because I wasn't man enough to say how I felt. I do love you. With all my heart."

"Lucius—"

"Let me finish. I've waited too long to say this and I won't let it sit any longer. I've always believed certain things about myself and what I should do, who I should be. Because of those, and a failed marriage that had more to do with being a failure at marriage than love, I didn't think my life could be any different than it was. Then along came you, with your teasing, your smile…" he squeezed her hands "…and your bright outlook on life. And I saw it could be amazing. The only problem was, I was afraid. Gut-wrenchingly afraid. What if I loved you and you didn't love me back? Or I lost that love?"

"That would never happen." Her heart hurt for the pain he'd been through.

"I couldn't and can't live without you. You are my life. You are what makes the sun shine in the morning and the moon bright at night for me. I have a few things I want to make clear. If it comes down to a choice between you and the baby, I will always pick you. If it's between you and me, I'll save you. If I have to give up the clinic to be with you, I will. If it is between you and medicine, I choose you. If it means living in Atlanta to have you, then that's what I'll do. I want *you*."

She threw her arms around him, moisture filling her eyes. "I want you too. And now it's my turn to express how I feel." She stood and tugged on his hand. "That can better be done in my bedroom."

Lucius grinned and followed her.

She stopped beside the bed. "I've missed you so much…" She began unbuttoning his shirt.

"Are you sure this is okay? I don't want to hurt the baby."

Amanda giggled. "Lucius, you're the smartest and most educated man I know—you know better than that."

"That may be true, but being a man in love with the woman carrying his child trumps all that knowledge."

"Dr. Lucius West, if you don't start taking my clothes off I'm going to hurt you."

She kissed him even while her hands went to his belt buckle.

Later that evening Lucius held Amanda in his arms as they lay in bed talking, and then kissing, then talking some more. This was what was truly important in life. He'd found real contentment for the first time. Amanda would always be by his side and his strongest supporter. Nothing else would ever matter. All the past had been washed away and he finally had a new start.

"I went to see my father the other day."

She turned so she could look at him. "And what happened?"

"To my surprise, a great deal. He told me that he'd learned too late that work isn't everything. That he had regrets where his family was concerned. That he wished he'd done some things differently. He made me see the light, so to speak."

"I'm really thankful for that." She kissed his shoulder.

"It's too late for my father and me to be close, but I'm going make sure my child knows I love him or her and that I'll be proud of them no matter what."

"I have no doubt you will. You make me feel very loved. I've had a revelation of my own. I had lunch with my mother and I learned that my stepfather isn't the person I thought. He cared about me but I just pushed him away—to a point from which it was hard to come back. I went for a visit this last weekend and apologized to him."

"That couldn't have been easy. I should have been there with you."

She kissed him. "You really are a nice guy."

"Don't sound so surprised." He grinned and ran his fingers over her ribs.

"I'm not—I promise. With my stepfather I managed. We hugged. Things aren't perfect, but at least in the future I'll be trying to meet him halfway."

"That's all anyone can ask. Hey, I meant to ask you…where are you flying to?"

"Sydney."

"Sydney?"

She laughed. "Yes—you know…where you live. I was coming back to you."

His eyes widened with wonder. "You were?"

"I was. I decided that even though you hadn't *said* you loved me you had already shown me you did in so many ways. That it wasn't fair to ask you to be someone you aren't."

His eyes twinkled. "So I wasted this trip?"

"I can make it worth your trouble." Amanda slid over and up him, giving him a deep, wet kiss.

Lucius's arms went around her. Yeah, he would be glad he'd gone to the trouble.

As they lay satiated, sometime later, Lucius placed his hand over the place where his baby grew, protected by Amanda.

"I brought you a stuffed koala bear. It's in my bag. You should have seen the looks I got as I came through Customs."

"I think I'll share it with the baby." She placed her hand over his. "I've already gotten what I really want from Australia."

Lucius kissed her behind the ear. "Would you like a girl or a boy?"

"I don't care. I just want him or her to be healthy and to have your blue eyes." She giggled. "The 'Baby Whisperer' strikes again."

"This time I'll proudly accept the title." He placed his lips against her ear. "I was just wondering if you would consider becoming Mrs. Lucius West? I love you from here to eternity and I always will."

She kissed him. "I would love to be your wife. That, and your love, and our baby, is all I'll ever need."

* * * * *

If you missed the previous story in the Miracles in the Making duet, look out for

Risking Her Heart on the Single Dad
by Annie O'Neil

And if you enjoyed this story, check out these other great reads from Susan Carlisle

Firefighter's Unexpected Fling
Highland Doc's Christmas Rescue
The Sheikh Doc's Marriage Bargain
Nurse to Forever Mom

All available now!